THE
SCHEME

THE
SCHEME

by Amethyst Drake

For Derald~

I finished my book.

Prologue

"Sorry I won't be able to make it home this weekend, Dad. I've got a ton of research on my desk and the books are due Monday." Olivia glanced at the pile of open library books on her desk to assure herself she wasn't completely lying.

"I understand, sweetheart. I'll look forward to next weekend even more. Go make the world a better place."

"Thanks, Dad. Love you!" Even though she enjoyed her weekly visits with her father, Olivia was glad to end the call.

This weekend she had plans of her own. Plans her father would never approve. She felt guilty for going behind his back, but what else could she do?

My desk is a mess, Olivia chided herself. She'd finished with the books yesterday but hadn't returned them because of her last-minute plans. Now, she didn't have time to tidy up. The silver framed picture of her mother and father caught her eye. She picked it up and fingered the frame. Remembering her mom always warmed her heart.

Mom would have understood. This was something Olivia had to do, even if it would hurt her father.

A knock at the door pulled her out of her memories. She replaced the photo and went to the door.

"I'm almost ready!"

"No rush," the tall, thin man said.

"Would you grab my things?" Olivia pointed to the blue suitcase beside her desk as she hurried into the bathroom. She ran a comb through her hair, switched off the lights, and grabbed her purse from the table by the sofa.

"Okay, let's go!" Olivia was eager to get started on her journey. She glanced at her father's face in the photo on her desk one last time. Then, she switched off the last light and locked the door carefully behind her.

1

"My daughter is missing." The businessman projected poise and confidence despite his agitation. He had a clean-shaved face, light tan complexion, and sparkling hazel eyes. His tailored suit fit his tall, muscular frame perfectly.

Katherine Carson had seen Jonathan Ames' picture in many entrepreneur magazines over the past decade and read about his multi-million-dollar company, Ames Enterprises. She never expected to be hosting the CEO in her comfy-but-cramped office. A businessman as important as Mr. Ames would have an army of personal security, lawyers, and investigators on permanent retainer. But here he was visiting a small private detective agency early on a Monday morning.

"Have you spoken to the police?" she asked.

"Yes, of course. They sent an officer to her apartment, but he didn't find anything."

"And your own security people?"

"My security detail has their hands full after the financial misconduct disclosure last year."

"I heard about that."

"You and everyone else. Anyway, my team is tied up with the new security protocols and continuing the audit. Besides, they are all based in Wilmington, Delaware. I want someone local investigating Olivia's whereabouts."

Katherine nodded her head and picked up a pen. "In that case, tell me about Olivia. When did you last see her, and when did she go missing?"

"Olivia is 24. She's a graduate student at Johns Hopkins University. We rang in 2009 together a couple weeks ago… that's the last time I saw her. But I've talked to her several times since then. She usually comes home to Delaware on the weekends. On Friday, Olivia called to say she would be busy with her research and wouldn't be able to come home."

"Is that unusual?"

"Yes, but this project is so important to her. I didn't think much of it. Then I had a business meeting come up here in Baltimore. I called Olivia to see if she was available for dinner after my meeting, but she didn't answer. I left a voice message and asked her to call me back. I called again Saturday evening…still no answer. I chalked it up to her being deep into her research. I decided to stop by her apartment after my meeting to see if she could take a break for dinner.

"Her car was in the parking lot where it usually is. But when I knocked, she didn't answer. I tried several times and spoke to her neighbors. I finally used my key to go inside to check on her. She wasn't in the apartment and her suitcase was gone." Mr. Ames stopped and looked at the detective expectantly.

Katherine blinked her deep blue eyes twice and resisted the urge to put her face in her hands. She put down the pen and clasped her fingers. "Is that all?"

"Yes. My daughter is missing and I want you to find her."

As a former Espionage Services operative, Katherine had years of experience in reading people. But it didn't take a highly trained agent to see the worry and determination in the father's eyes. She chose her next words with care. "Mr. Ames, I appreciate your concern for your daughter. Is it possible she just wanted to spend the weekend with friends and didn't want to hurt your feelings?"

"No. She's spent weekends with friends before. But never without telling me. What reason could she have for deceiving me?" Mr. Ames brought his fist down firmly on the desk to emphasize the word 'reason.'

Katherine sensed he was trying to convince himself as much as her. "You don't seem sure of that."

Mr. Ames sighed and ran a hand through his thick brown hair. "There could be one reason for her to go off without telling me anything."

Katherine stood to refill her glass at the water cooler. She didn't see how she could help Mr. Ames, but she could tell there was more to his story. Probably a lot more. She offered Mr. Ames some water before asking him to tell her the rest.

"For the last year or so, Olivia has been seeing a young man, Robert Norton. I don't like him. There's something shifty about him that I can't quite put my finger on."

"I see. Is the relationship serious?"

Mr. Ames' jaw tightened. "Recently they have been talking about marriage."

"Quite serious, then. What do find objectionable about him?"

"Everything. First of all, he's nearly 30, but he is just now going for his bachelor's degree. He says he served in the Navy, and that's why his degree got delayed. But I don't believe him."

"Why not?" Katherine had started serving her country before completing a traditional education. So, she didn't see anything particularly suspicious in that.

"Well, for one thing he is far too unreliable for a Navy man. And based on what little information I've been able to pry out of him, his knowledge of naval protocol is about as deep as a puddle."

"I assume you've served then?"

"Yes, proudly. I thought we'd be able to swap stories, get to know each other. But Robert is downright evasive. I've tried to be welcoming every time he comes home with her. I ask a lot of questions, but he's been dating my daughter for a year. I hardly know anything about him."

"You think he is trying to take advantage of her?"

"I think he's after her allowance, or her inheritance. I've told Olivia my concerns, but she's completely smitten and will not listen to reason."

"You think he convinced her to go away with him?" She remembered how it felt to be smitten beyond all reason, although her father wasn't around to protest.

"I don't want to believe it. Olivia is independent, strong, self-sufficient. But I'm afraid my refusal to accept her boyfriend may have driven her to do something... impulsive."

"I'm still not sure what you want me to do for you, Mr. Ames. If your daughter left her apartment willingly, she'll contact you when she's ready."

"Yes, but what if Robert is a conman? What if she was tricked and now she's in trouble."

"You think foul play is involved?"

"Yes! Even if she were going to marry against my wishes, I would have heard from her—something—by now. What if he is holding her against her will, or keeping her from contacting me? The police couldn't find a criminal record on Robert, but I'm still not convinced." Mr. Ames pulled a handkerchief out of his jacket pocket.

"I'm surprised you didn't use your considerable clout to pressure them into investigating."

"Believe me, I tried." He wiped his forehead and put the handkerchief back in his pocket. "I even spoke to the commissioner of police. In this instance, I'm afraid our social standing serves only to convince the police my spoiled rich girl has 'run away from home.' But I tell you she is not that kind of girl. And yet, it's been days since I've heard from her."

"Have you considered approaching the media? Get her name and picture out to the public?"

Mr. Ames shifted in his seat. "Ms. Carson, I really need to find my daughter. I also need to keep the publicity to a minimum while the fraud investigation is ongoing. And I worry about what might happen to Olivia if Robert sees her on the news."

"Mr. Ames, I wish I could give you some peace of mind, but this isn't the type of case we normally take on." In fact, Carson Investigations got most of its cases from local criminal defense lawyers. It was one way that Katherine was able to keep herself emotionally detached from the cases.

"I know your reputation, Ms. Carson. But I also know you are the best private detective in the city. The commissioner himself recommended you to me."

She chuckled. "I doubt that..."

"Well, he may have told me it would be a waste of money to hire a private detective. But he did say if I insisted on wasting my money, I couldn't do better than to waste it on you."

Katherine clapped her hands together. "Now that sounds more like Harrison!"

Mr. Ames smiled. "I may be an over protective father who forced my daughter to go behind my back to get married. I hope I am being paranoid. In any case, I'm willing to pay you double your usual fee to find my daughter ... no matter what the outcome is."

Katherine paused. Ordinarily, she would never consider a case on its financial merit. But last year's economic downturn changed things. People were already calling it the "Great Recession of 2008." So, a paying client was an asset no small business owner could afford to turn away.

She sighed. "All right, Mr. Ames. We'll find your daughter. Let me get some information from you to give us a place to start."

2

The Carson Investigations office didn't keep regular hours. Instead, Katherine sent a text to the other members of her team as soon as she accepted the new case.

"Client briefing in 30."

Three replies pinged back almost immediately. Katherine had intentionally left out any information about the case in her message. She knew her team well enough to expect disapproval and wanted a chance to convince them in person. Katherine did a quick internet search on the names she'd gotten from Mr. Ames while she waited.

Jake was the first to arrive, as usual. Punctuality was one of many traits that made him successful in his former career at the National Security Agency. His black eyes, strong nose, and dark beige skin gave him a rugged, striking appeal. He went straight to the small coffee station in one corner of the room and filled the coffee maker with water.

"Morning, Katie. Your new haircut looks good." Jake filled a coffee filter with a heaping scoop of Folgers and slid the brew basket into place.

"Thanks, Jake." Katherine flipped her brown shoulder length layers. "How'd it go yesterday?"

"As well as expected." Jake hung his jacket on a coat hook and pulled off his toboggan, revealing a dark black crew cut. "The DA sends his regards."

"Well, that's something."

They went over a few more details of the unfortunate Philips' investigation. The net result of which was a plea bargain and three weeks of unpaid overtime. Jake wrapped up the conversation as the deep, earthy scent of fresh-brewed coffee filled the air. "We did the right thing, Katie."

"Yeah. I just wish I'd realized Mr. Philips was guilty before we took the case."

"I'm glad you can still see the good in people after everything you've been through."

Sammi walked in the door before Katherine could respond. "Buenos días, everyone! Hey, Jakey, save some coffee for me!"

Sammi ripped off her coat and scarf and threw them on the back of the sofa. Jake used his seven extra inches of height to hold his mug out of reach. Sammi grabbed the cinnamon and tried to convince him to spice up his black coffee. Watching the pair interact made Katherine chuckle. Ever since she'd been hired as an administrative assistant to the detectives, Samantha Maria Garcia had been treating "Jakey" like her little brother. They both seemed to ignore the twenty-year age gap between them.

A few minutes later, Lee came into the room wrapped from earmuffs to boots in heavy layers. His usually fair skin was pink with cold. Even after years living in the north, Lee couldn't adjust to frigid weather. The Georgia native hung his winter gear on two coat hooks. He tousled his dirty blonde hair, which was at least three weeks overdue for a trim.

With everyone present, Katherine asked her team to huddle up. Sammi flopped down on one of the two sofas that served as their conference room and receiving area. Jake sat on the other sofa. Lee grabbed a chair and straddled it backwards, resting his arms on the backrest. Katherine sat on the other end of Jake's sofa, dropping a file folder with her case notes on the coffee table. After she summarized her meeting with their new client, Jake was the first to speak up.

"I'm not even sure we have a case here, Katherine."

"Yeah, I'm sorry for Señor Ames, but his daughter is a grown woman. It feels…icky to be poking into her business." Sammi tapped her foot and twirled a long strand of brunette hair through her fingers.

"If the boyfriend is a conman, the police would've turned up something on him," Lee reasoned. "I reckon Mr. Ames is just suffering from an overactive imagination."

"You all make valid points. But the bottom line is this: Mr. Ames has hired us to find his daughter. Period."

Jake crossed his arms, Lee scowled, and Sammi sat bolt upright. Katherine held her hands up to quiet the grumbling before it could begin. "This case is every bit as important as any of our others. Our job is to find out where she is, even if there is no bad guy, and even if she left of her own free will."

"Are we taking this case because our client is rich?"

"Yes, Sammi, and to give Mr. Ames peace of mind. I can't keep this agency afloat on clients who can't pay. But Mr. Ames has generously offered to pay us double our usual fee, no matter what we learn. We only have to find where this girl is, let her dad know, and that will be that. Minimal effort. Easy paycheck."

"Understood." Jake stood and stretched his arms. "Where do we start?"

"I'd like you to reach out to your contacts on the police force. Find out who took Mr. Ames' call before he ran it up to the commissioner. Go over the background check on the boyfriend. See if they missed any red flags. And get an address so we can try to interview him. His name is Robert Norton. I couldn't find anything about him online, so we'll have to get intel the old-fashioned way."

"Does Ames really think Norton is the reason his daughter went missing?" As a former NSA Intelligence Analyst, Lee liked getting more details. His friend Jake was already out the door to work on his assignment.

"He believes Norton is some sort of con artist. Ames Enterprises is worth millions of dollars, and Olivia is the only heir."

"Money can be a powerful motivator. How do he and his daughter get along?"

"He says they've had a close relationship until recently, since Norton entered the picture. He's upset because Olivia has never lied to him before."

"At least as far as he knew."

Katherine nodded. "This time she claimed she was staying home to study, but…"

"Wonder what really happened." Lee scratched his ear.

"That's what we're going to find out. We have a witness of sorts. Mr. Ames talked with one of Olivia's neighbors, a Mrs. Nichols. She's an older lady, works at the campus library. She may have seen Robert come into the building that night, but she's not sure."

"Well, it's something to start with anyway. Want me to check on Mrs. Nichols? Maybe see if the apartment building has any security cameras?" Lee moved his chair back to its original position against the wall.

"You read my mind. That's exactly what I want you to do. Also, check out Olivia's car. Sammi, I want you to dig into Olivia's digital life. See if she's on social media. Check where she's been surfing, who she's been in contact with in the last week or so, and whether her online patterns have changed."

Sammi slumped and made a face. Katherine handed her a sleek leather case and lifted her eyebrows. "I know what you think of this, dear. But her father gave me her laptop and a list of passwords. If she were as concerned about privacy as you, she wouldn't have given him those, would she?"

Sammi huffed. "I guess not. I'll see what I can find." She took the laptop case and headed for one of the desks at the back of the room.

"So, is Norton our only lead?" Lee asked as he started to layer his jackets. "What about friends and family?"

"We can't rule out anything at this point. As far as family goes, Mr. Ames says they don't have any to speak of. Only a niece and nephew he hasn't spoken to in years. Sounds like they resent him for being rich and not doing more to support them when their mother died."

"Should be easy enough to confirm. Where will you be?" Lee threw the end of his scarf over his shoulder.

"I've got a lunch meeting. Then, I'm going to campus to track down her friends and teachers. They were closest to Olivia in her daily life."

"We should check into security footage on campus as well."

"Yes, hopefully we can piece together her movements on Friday. Here, Mr. Ames gave us a recent picture to work with."

Lee examined the framed 8 by 10 glossy. The photo was taken about six weeks ago, at Thanksgiving. Olivia and her father posed back-to-back, looking into the camera. Olivia was only a couple inches shorter than her father. Her eyes sparkled with the same energy as his. Her long brown hair was tucked attractively behind one ear and pinned with a sunflower. Her bright smile went all the way to her big brown eyes.

"A smile full of kindness," Lee said. "Just the kind of girl to be taken in by a con artist."

Sammi piped up, "Maybe she was kidnapped!"

"Unlikely…Kidnappers would have called or sent a ransom note by now." Lee laughed as Sammi stuck out her lower lip in a mock pout.

"Tell you what, Sammi," Katherine said with a smile. "After we've exhausted all the other possibilities, we'll look into your theory. But for now, we're sticking to the facts we have."

3

Katherine drove her Ford Focus to Miss Shirley's Café on West Cold Spring Lane. Despite the cold, gloomy day, the diner was bustling as usual. Mr. Ames had arranged for her to have a lunch meeting with George Murphy, Dean of the Medical Faculty at Johns Hopkins. Katherine circled the building to park in the restaurant's small lot. Entering the rear door, she was assaulted by a cloud of sound—the clinking of dishes and chatter of patrons. A bookish man with fair skin and balding silver hair sat alone at a booth in the front of the restaurant with reading glasses on the end of his nose. Katherine navigated the maze of tables and chairs to cross the room.

"Dean Murphy? My name is Katherine Carson."

"You must be the detective Jonathan hired! He asked me to cooperate in any way I can." The dean stood to shake her hand. His grip was firm and steady, and his body language indicated he was comfortable with his position and accustomed to working with people. "Please, have a seat. I've just been perusing the menu. Everything here looks delicious."

Katherine ordered a ham and cheese croissant melt without looking at the menu. She knew what she liked. She tapped her foot to the beat of the local radio station playing in the background. Dean Murphy asked the waitress several questions before ordering the chicken pot pie skillet.

"Now," Murphy said with a satisfied sigh. "How can I be of help to your investigation?"

"I'd like to get some information about Olivia's performance as a student. I understand you two are close?"

"I've been friends with Jonathan Ames for years. We studied together at Harvard. I was best man at his wedding and I'm Olivia's godfather."

"It must be gratifying to have your goddaughter studying with you at Johns Hopkins." Katherine knew how happy her own godparents were to have her living in Baltimore.

"Yes, indeed! We have one of the top medical research facilities in the country, if I do say so myself. And Olivia—it's been a pleasure to watch her grow and blossom. She has one of the finest minds I have ever worked with. She is going to revolutionize research in her field!"

"What field is that?"

"Bio-printing. More specifically, Olivia and her research partners are researching the potential use of bio-printed organs in human transplant operations."

Katherine raised her eyebrows. "That sounds…"

"Like science fiction?" Murphy chuckled. "It was, ten years ago. But now we have the technology to create bio-ink using living cells and bio-materials. Then we can theoretically use that bio-ink to 'print' a functioning organ."

"You're talking about manufacturing human organs in a lab to be used in place of organ donors?"

"Precisely. It's no secret there is a disgraceful shortage of organ donors compared to the number of people who need transplant surgery. Imagine if medical science could provide the solution. The potential applications are endless!"

Katherine thanked the waitress who delivered their food. She listened to the Dean ramble on about his favorite subject while she bit into her cheesy sandwich. It was so hot it nearly burnt her tongue. She enjoyed picking up obscure knowledge from people talking about their areas of expertise. Several minutes later, she pulled the Dean back to the real purpose of their meeting.

"Could you tell me a little more about Olivia?"

"Oh, of course. Olivia is as passionate about this subject as I am. And she has the drive, initiative, and creativity to turn some of these theories into reality. Ever since her mother's death, she's been determined to find a way to produce artificial human organs. She died of renal disease, you know."

"No, I didn't know that." Katherine felt a pang of empathy as she made a note in her pad.

"Yes. Terrible thing. She died before she could obtain a viable organ for transplant. Olivia was twelve at the time." The Dean ate a forkful of chicken and wiped his mouth. "Then, of course, Olivia's aunt passed away a few years before her mother, from complications after her body rejected a transplant organ. So, you can see why this field would be important to Olivia."

"Yes, I can relate. My own childhood tragedies have motivated much of my career." Katherine pushed down memories of her past by pressing forward. "What kind of woman is Olivia? From my conversation with Mr. Ames, I got the impression they are very close. Do you believe she might have gone off some-where on her own, without telling him?"

"I've never met a man who loves his daughter as much as Jonathan loves Olivia. And Olivia is devoted to him. I can't imagine her leaving town without letting her father know. And she would not, under any circumstances, leave her research. No one could ever manipulate her into that."

"I see Mr. Ames has shared his theory with you."

"Yes, he expressed his concern that she fell victim to a con artist. Or at least ran off to get married. I can't speak to how serious her relationship was. I never met Robert. But it's hard to believe Olivia would go behind her father's back."

"So, you don't agree that Olivia's relationship with her boyfriend has affected her in some way." Katherine took the final bite of her delicious sandwich.

"Now, I didn't say that either. She got perfect scores through-out her undergraduate studies. Outstanding performance and top of every class. She had near-perfect scores during her first year in the graduate program as well. This past year, though, her grades have been slipping."

"You mean she's failing?" Katherine pushed her empty plate away and wiped her mouth with a napkin.

"No, no! Not slipping that much. It's just that she's been distracted since she started seeing Robert, and it shows." Dean Murphy nodded gravely.

"I understand that Robert is an undergraduate student in the engineering department?"

"I believe so, although I am not as familiar with students enrolled in other departments. You should talk to Mary Yoseff, the Assistant Dean of Academic Advising. She would know more about his program."

Katherine wrote the name in her notebook. "Okay. Who else is Olivia close to?"

Murphy took another bite while he thought. "She's probably closest to her research partners, Donna Applegate and Gordon Jones. I know she and Donna are friends. She has a rivalry of sorts with Gordon. The three are working together on the research for their graduate program. Olivia is outshining him, but competition keeps everyone sharp. Their thesis advisor is Dr. Kevin Mahoney. Other than that, I'm not sure."

Katherine glanced at her watch and started to wrap up the interview. "Is there anything else you think I should know?"

"Yes." Murphy pointed his for at Katherine. "The bio-engineering department has open lab time from 10:00 a.m. to 10:00 p.m. on Tuesdays. This is a time when students meet to share notes, ask questions, and collaborate. I can't be sure where Olivia is today, but I can guarantee that she will show up there tomorrow, if she is at all able."

"That's very helpful to know, Dean Murphy. Thank you for your time and cooperation."

"It was a pleasure meeting you, detective. I do hope you are able to locate Olivia and set Jonathan's mind at ease."

Sammi was not happy about the new case. Not at all. First because they were working for the uber-privileged one percent. And she was expected to invade Olivia's personal life because she might be defying her father's wishes. The whole thing left a bad taste in her mouth. *If I ran the agency, I would never have taken this case.*

But Sammi was far from the top of the ladder in this business. Katherine, Lee, and Jake had years of experience in what they called the 'intelligence community.' Sammi called it spying. That was before they'd started the detective agency together seven years ago. Sammi had graduated just two years ago with her BS in Criminal Justice from the University of Baltimore. One of her favorite adjunct professors had introduced her to Katherine and she became her administrative assistant a little over a year ago. *If Professor Mitchell could see me now.* She sighed as she started pulling up popular social media sites. She was supposed to search Olivia's laptop, but she had no intention of digging deeper than necessary.

Selfie. Selfie. Book review. Sammi's mind wandered as she scrolled through Olivia's public Myspace profile. The steady sounds of traffic driving past the building began to lull her back to sleep. *All I do is phone calls and research.*

She shifted her attention to Olivia's Facebook page. More and more people were switching to the new social media platform to connect with friends. Unlike her Myspace page, Olivia's Facebook was set to private. Sammi could only see public profile pictures and a few friends with public profiles. As she scrolled, she thought about her own friends, both here and back home in Puerto Rico. She'd moved in with her aunt and uncle when she decided to pursue her dream of becoming a detective. Early on, her dream had been fueled by TV crime drama. Then she'd discovered a passion for solving mysteries and helping people find answers.

Sammi shut down the computer browser with a sigh. She eyed the laptop case on the coffee table, but shook her head. Crossing her arms, she decided it was time to change tactics.

4

Jake began his search for a suspect where he always did. At least, ever since setting up shop as a private detective in Charm City. During his years as an operator, Jake had made contacts in police departments across the country. But most of his intel would come from intelligence analysts like Lee.

Now, he contacted one of his many friends at the Baltimore Police Department. He wanted to speak to a young cop whose beat would include the neighborhood around JHU. He learned that Officer Dylan Burgess wasn't on duty today. So, Jake headed to the Uptown Boxing Center where he knew his friend would be on his day off.

The Center was a large open space with two boxing rings in the middle of the room. Around the perimeter, rows of heavy bags showed the scars of countless punches thrown in rage and resolve. The air smelled of testosterone and sweat. A half dozen pairs of athletes sparred. Others did cardio and core workouts. Near the back wall, a muscular young man pummeled a hundred pound heavy bag. Jake grabbed a towel as he made his way through the room.

"Hey, Champ!" Jake tossed the towel to Dylan.

"Hey, Cap. Here for a little exercise?"

"Not today. I'm looking for some information."

Officer Burgess grinned as he wiped sweat off his shaved head and deep brown shoulders. "Yeah, that's probably best for an old man like you. Ask away."

Jake cocked an eyebrow but did not give in to the younger man's challenge. "Did you hear about Jonathan Ames contacting the police department this weekend?"

"Hear about it? Cap, I was on duty when his first call came in. A buddy of mine is the one who got assigned to go out to her apartment. I doubt they woulda sent him 'cept her daddy is so rich." Dylan flipped the towel over his shoulder and took a gulp from his water bottle.

"I heard about his call to Commissioner Harrison."

"Yeah, calls, plural. The man was crazy with worry. Least that's what my buddy says."

"But he did go to the apartment?" Jake held the bag steady.

"Oh, yeah he went, after Ames called the commissioner down on us. Courtesy to a fine upstanding citizen, yada, yada. Dude doesn't even live in this state." Dylan crouched and began sparring with the bag again.

"Guessing your buddy didn't find anything to investigate."

"Nope. Aside from Ames' worry, nothing was out of place. No signs of forced entry. Nada. Ames even admitted that her suitcase was gone." Dylan jabbed right, left, right.

"So, the assumption is that she ran away."

"Cap, the assumption is that a grown-ass woman can go wherever she wants without her daddy knowing about it."

Jake tilted his head in agreement. "Keep your chin tucked, Champ." He felt a swell of pride. Dylan had grown into a strong man. He had served his country in the Army and now continued his service on the police force. Jake knew Dylan's father would have been proud as well. When Dylan finished his bag work, they walked together to the cardio room.

"I need to head out, Champ. One more question. Do you know anything about Robert Norton?"

"Nope." Dylan refilled his water bottle and took a long drink. "He's not in the system. Why you so interested in this?"

"Apparently, Harrison put him on to hiring a detective ..."

"Sucks to be you then."

"Yeah, well. Thanks for the encouragement, Champ." Jake slapped his friend on the shoulder.

"Anytime, Cap. Anytime."

Lee scanned the aging exterior of the apartment building. Dark clouds covered the late-morning sun, making the plain brick structure across the street from JHU student housing seem even more dreary.

The parking lot was mostly empty. It didn't take long to spot Olivia's 2009 gray Volvo and confirm the license plate number. Lee checked the door handles. Locked. He jammed his hands in his coat pockets and peered in through the closed windows. The interior of the car was clean and clutter-free. The only item visible was a big purple bag on the floor in the back seat.

Lee stooped to check inside the wheel wells and found a small metallic box near the rear tire. *Too easy.* He removed the spare key and stood up with a groan. His stiff knees reminded him his fortieth birthday was only a couple years away. He opened the rear door and leaned in to rummage through the tote bag. It contained a hair dryer, brush, and assorted grooming tools and hair accessories. Lee smirked. *Women and their hair.*

Climbing into the driver's seat, he cranked the engine and

recorded the mileage and gas level. He checked the cup holders, sun visor, and center console which held a red fold-away umbrella. Finally, he reached across to open the glove box. Inside was the manufacture's guide, car registration, insurance, and a small notebook.

Lee put everything back except the notebook. Pages of notes listed medical suppliers, doctors, and hospitals with checked-off phone numbers. The last page of text had one phone number and the name Meg Russell. He texted the number to Sammi. It still felt odd to delegate research tasks, but he wasn't complaining. He'd left the NSA to get away from tedious research, among other things.

The frigid wind nearly took his breath away as he walked up to the heavy front door. Inside, the gray hallway was lined with wood panel doors. An old plastic security camera was stuck to the ceiling in the far back corner. *So much for surveillance.*

Lee knocked on the door of apartment 116, located directly beneath Olivia's apartment. A woman with rosy skin and gray curls pulled the door open until the security chain caught.

"Yes?" She peered at the intruder, clutching the collar of a pink bathrobe to her chest.

Lee flashed his most winning smile. He pulled his credentials out of his pocket and held them so the woman could see. "Mrs. Nichols, I'm a private detective hired to find your upstairs neighbor, Olivia Ames."

The woman didn't budge. She took her time reading the license in his wallet. Lee swallowed back the impulse to ask her to get her reading glasses. Then she turned her bright green eyes onto the tall detective, looking him up and down. She nodded curtly and pushed the door closed.

5

Lee took a step back as the door closed in his face. Being the charming one of the team, he was used to being able to get his foot in the door. Especially with the ladies. He debated about postponing the interview with Mrs. Nichols while he searched Olivia's apartment upstairs. But he knew Kat would want to join him for the search. Lee raised his hand to knock again. Then he heard the screech of something being dragged across the floor coming from inside Mrs. Nichols apartment.

"Mrs. Nichols?" Lee pressed his ear to the door. *What the ...?* He heard a cacophony of sounds from inside. Drawers being slammed. The clatter of dishes being moved about. He knocked. A cat yowled. *What am I getting myself into?*

"Quiet, Fluffy!"

"Mrs. Nichols? Are you alright?" He knocked louder as he became concerned for the woman's safety.

"Just a minute!" She called out in a sing-song voice.

More crashes and bumps. Finally, the sound of the door chain being unbolted. Then, footsteps hurried away.

"Come in!" sang the voice.

Unsure of himself, Lee glanced both ways down the hall-way before nudging the door open. Bookshelves lined every wall of the small room. An old green couch was pushed up against a row of bookshelves on the back wall. The only small window was partially obscured by the couch and bookcases. An orange tabby cat perched on the back of the sofa. Mrs. Nichols sat on a red velvet captain's chair positioned at an angle to the couch.

"Would you care for some tea?" She held a blue and white tea cup in her hand.

Lee blinked, trying to take everything in. "Thank you, Mrs. Nichols."

"Oh, please, dear. I'm not married anymore. Call me Ms."

Lee blinked again as he carefully stepped around the un-suitably large coffee table to sit on the low green couch. Aside from being crowded, the tiny apartment appeared clean and well kept.

Mrs., that is, Ms. Nichols had miraculously changed from her bathrobe into a brown suit and green blouse. She had laid out tea and cookies on the coffee table and insisted on serving her guest.

"Thank you." Lee said as his mother's voice echoed in his memory. *A gentleman always receives hospitality with grati-tude.* He smiled. His hostess added a lot of cream and three sugar cubes to his tea. Then, she gave him a plate of cookies.

"Now ..." Ms. Nichols sat back in her chair with a satisfied sigh. "Tell me more about yourself."

"My name is Lee Stewart. I'm a private detective. I—"

"You mentioned that. Is Lee short for Leroy?"

"No, ma'am, not as far as I know." Lee took a big bite of a chocolate chip cookie.

"Oh, I'm sure it is. People are always shortening their perfectly good names. Do you rock climb, Leroy?"

"Uh...no. I don't." *A great start to the interview.*

"Such a pity! Rock climbing is good for the mind and body. You should try it sometime."

Lee set down his teacup, untouched. "Yes, ma'am. I was hoping —"

"Now, tell me, Leroy, what can I do for a private detective." Ms. Nichols wiggled her eyebrows when she said *private detective.* "I'm certainly glad they sent you and not one of those police detectives. Last time I ran into one of them they were none too polite, let me tell you."

"I'm sorry to hear that. I was wonder—"

"Of course, you're here because dear Olivia is missing. Her father was raising a ruckus over the weekend to find her."

"Yes, we are trying to find out what happened."

"Who's we, dear?" Ms. Nichols leaned forward to place her elbow at the end of the arm rest and balanced her head on her fist, like a diminutive Thinker.

Lee caught a whiff of jasmine perfume which he was sure she was not wearing when she first opened the door.

"My agency. That is, the detective agency I work for. Carson Investigations." Lee was accustomed to being relaxed and composed, but felt inexplicably nervous under the scrutiny of the older woman.

"Carson Investigations. Hmm, and your name's Stewart. Not the boss then?" Ms. Nichols reached for her tea cup and added another lump of sugar.

"No, I have two partners. We're named after Katherine Carson." Lee would have chosen something more generic, but he'd been outvoted.

"Oh my, is it hard for her being a female PI?"

"I've actually never thought about that, but she gets the job done. Our other partner is a man. And so am I."

Ms. Nichols looked up from her tea. "I can see that."

Lee shifted uncomfortably and cleared his throat. "Ms. Nichols, I do have some ques—"

"Oh, yes, of course!" Ms. Nichols put down her teacup and folded her hands in her lap. "First, you'll want to know where I was when Olivia went missing. I was right here, in my apartment, with Fluffy, from 6:00 pm on through the night. Yes, I did notice something odd about 7:00 pm. A man parked illegally in the alley below my window and entered the building. He climbed the hill and went upstairs. No, I didn't see or talk to Olivia after I got home, although I did see her at the library earlier in the day. I didn't notice anything strange about her behavior, but I do think it's possible that Olivia and Robert would elope. Any other questions?"

During this monologue, Lee had been scanning the large bookshelves. He noticed two shelves of books fully dedicated to the works of Agatha Christie. He deliberately chose to close his eyes a moment rather than roll them.

"Uh, yes. Where did you say that you saw Olivia last?"

"At the library on campus. I work there almost every day. Olivia volunteers with us three days a week."

"You aren't working today?" Lee asked.

"The library is open late on Mondays and I take the one to ten shift. As I was saying, Olivia was at the library on Friday morning and nothing seemed out of the ordinary."

"Do you know what her plans were for the evening?"

"She had a standing lunch date with Robert on Fridays after her shift. And she was still planning on going to see her father over the weekend as she always did. I didn't know she changed her plans until Mr. Ames came barreling in with a police officer on Sunday. He was very worried. I felt so bad for him, but I didn't want to accuse Robert of anything."

"Have you met Robert?"

"Yes." Ms. Nichols moved to sit on the couch, displacing Fluffy from his favorite perch.

Lee found himself uncomfortably sandwiched between the jasmine scented librarian and the fat orange cat. Fluffy purred loudly.

Ms. Nichols whispered, "Do you agree with Mr. Ames that Robert is responsible? Or do you have other suspects?"

"We've only just started investigating, ma'am." Lee tried to lift the purring mass of fur onto his knee so he could slide further away from Ms. Nichols.

"Oh, Leroy, don't 'ma'am' me. I know all about Olivia and her beau. He seems like a nice young man. It's normal for fathers to be uptight about their daughters marrying. Especially an only child like Olivia."

"You think Mr. Ames' worries are unfounded?" Lee settled back into the sofa with Fluffy in his lap.

"Absolutely. Olivia is as sharp as a tack. She would never be taken in by a conman. Swept off her feet, of course! But never taken in."

Lee pondered the fine line that exists between being 'swept' and 'taken' as he stroked the cat in his lap. He had never found a woman that made him want to take the time to sweep her off her feet. He didn't think he took advantage of women. But he'd lost count of how many first dates he'd written off with a promise to call in the morning.

"Did Olivia talk about Robert much?"

"Oh, yes. She adored him. And of course, she would come in after a date at all hours of the night. She did her best to be quiet, but an old building like this has its own secrets to tell."

"You said you saw Robert here Friday night?"

"Not exactly." Ms. Nichols poured herself another cup of tea. "I said I saw a young man here Friday night."

"In that case, can you tell me exactly what happened?"

"As I said, it was about 7:00 pm. I had just finished washing my dishes and setting out my gear for the next day. I go hiking every weekend, Leroy. Fluffy was napping in his spot on the couch. Suddenly, he let out a yowl and jumped as we both heard the slam of a car door right outside the window!"

Ms. Nichols stood up so Lee could look out the window behind her. "That's a no parking zone in that alley. No parking, for any reason. But there he was, walking in like he owned the place. Scaring poor Fluffy. We chose this apartment specifically because of the location in the back where it would be quiet."

"Can you describe the man you saw?"

"It was dark and the alley is down the hill at an odd angle for me to see. And I was flustered. But the man was tall, about your height, and a little thinner than you. Although, I'm sure you'd lose a little weight if you hiked more. I couldn't see his face or hair, but I heard him bound up the stairs two at a time, which is why I thought he was young. It could have been almost anyone."

"Could it have been Robert?"

Ms. Nichols sighed and took a sip of her tea.

"I appreciate your information, Ms. Nichols. You never know when the smallest detail could be important. Perhaps something in the way he walked?"

"I'll tell you what I think, detective, but you must try to keep my secret. I don't want to upset her father. I haven't had much occasion to see Robert walk, but I do believe it was likely Robert I saw. And I do believe Olivia went with him."

"What makes you think so?" Lee leaned closer.

"Olivia had a hair appointment sometime that afternoon with a new hairstylist."

Lee stared blankly.

Ms. Nichols wagged her finger at him. "Trying a new hair stylist is a big change for a woman. She was excited about it!"

"Do you think it's related to her disappearance?"

"I think it's possible. Perhaps Olivia wanted to get her hair styled because it was a special occasion. A special occasion, like a wedding." Ms. Nichols inclined her head. "Her own wedding."

Lee wrinkled his brow. The suggestion was not impossible. He made a note to mention it to Katherine. "Didn't you say she told you she was going to her father's for the weekend as usual?"

"Yes. That's what she said. Ordinarily, of course, I would never think of accusing Olivia of lying, she's such a dear. But a girl in love..." She clasped her hands to her heart and sighed. "Who's to say what she'll do?"

"You believe Olivia is in love, then, and went away with Robert to get married."

Ms. Nichols blushed. "A secret romance is every woman's dream, Detective. I'm sure Olivia is alright. Her father will understand in time."

"One more thing. Did you hear or see Olivia leave the building? With or without the man?"

"I'm afraid I didn't. Thinking it was Robert going upstairs, I went into my room and turned on Masterpiece Theater. Then I fell asleep and didn't hear anything else."

"I see."

"I will also say, Leroy, I am not a heavy sleeper. Her place is directly above us, you know. If Olivia had been screaming, or if there was a fight, I would have heard."

Lee nodded his head. He believed her. "Thank you again, Ms. Nichols."

"Oh, detective! Let me give you my phone number in case you want to get in touch later."

"Of course, I'll let you know if I have any more questions."

"Call me anytime, Leroy, even if you don't have questions." Ms. Nichols winked.

Lee hurried outside to wait for Katherine in the safety of the parking lot.

6

Katherine pulled up to Olivia's apartment building and saw Lee using his scarf to swipe at his dark blue jacket. She snickered under her breath when she realized what he was doing.

"Did you pick up anything other than cat hair?" She patted him on the shoulder and plucked off a few orange hairs.

Lee shot her a lopsided grin. "Ms. Nichols is 62 years young and an adventurer in her spare time. She works on campus at the library and sees Olivia there all the time." Lee stuffed the scarf into a pocket and held open the door. "And get this. She saw Olivia Friday morning and Olivia told her she was planning to go to her father's like usual."

"Olivia could have been lying to her." Katherine followed Lee up the narrow staircase.

"That's what Ms. Nichols said. She thinks Olivia and Robert eloped because they are in love. But she can't be sure if he was the man who startled Fluffy with his car Friday night."

Katherine listened with interest as Lee filled her in on the rest of his interview. "Ms. Nichols sounds like a firecracker!"

"Yep." At the top of the stairs, Lee pointed out another fake security camera. "She also thinks Olivia's appointment with a new hairstylist is proof that she was planning to get married."

They reached the door of apartment number 216. Mr. Ames had told them where to find Olivia's spare key. Lee reached up and felt the top of the door frame. "No key. I guess Ames forgot to leave it."

"He has his own key. He just said Olivia keeps it up there." Katherine bent down to flip back the welcome mat. Still no key. She sighed. "Should we see if the manager has a spare?"

"The manager isn't on site." Lee slouched against the wall. "If only we knew someone who could pick a lock."

Katherine rolled her eyes, but smiled in spite of herself. "Breaking and entering could lose me my license." Lee and Jake liked to tease her about some of her skills, although they always stopped short of mentioning the Espionage Services Agency.

"Sure, sure. But we do have permission to enter. And we'd have to drive to Wilmington to get another key from Ames ..." Lee let his voice trail off and studied his fingernails.

Katherine chuckled and pulled out her pocket knife. "You know I don't carry picks anymore." She opened the knife and carefully slid the high carbon stainless steel blade between the door and the striker plate. Finding the latch, she pushed it out of the door jam and opened the door.

"Don't tell Sammi."

"Never." A huge grin spread over Lee's face.

The door creaked as she pushed it open. The fragrance of oranges and clove was evident as soon as they entered. The source of the smell, a bowl of dried orange pomanders, sat on a hall table. Around the corner, a small desk was positioned against a wall between the hall and kitchen door. Katherine admired the cozy living area. Instead of a TV, Olivia had rows of framed pictures of friends, family, and achievements. A single photograph sat on the desk. Katherine picked up the silver frame and looked at the smiling young couple holding hands. The man was obviously a young Jonathan Ames, and the woman closely resembled Olivia. Katherine showed the picture to Lee and told him what she'd learned from her interview with Dean Murphy about Olivia's mother.

"No wonder she's so interested in bio-printing human organs." Lee picked up a scale model of a kidney from the bookshelf and raised his eyebrows dramatically.

"No doubt. We always want to avenge our parents." She took a deep breath and allowed herself a moment of recollection about her parents' death in the line of duty. She set the picture down. The only other items on the desk were a full pencil holder and blank notepad. One shallow drawer beneath the desk held paperclips, colorful post-it notes, and a hole punch.

Katherine entered the bedroom and started searching Olivia's closet. She noticed several empty clothes hangers. "We don't know what clothes she owned, or what she might have taken with her, so I'm not sure how much help this will be for narrowing down where she went."

"Her laundry hamper is empty." Lee noted, moving on to search the dresser. "Look, here's some pictures she hasn't had a chance to put in frames."

Katherine took the photos from Lee. The first showed Olivia standing next to a pretty woman with dark curly hair and light brown skin. "Donna" was printed on the back.

"This is probably Donna Applegate that Dean Murphy mentioned. Here she is again with Olivia and a few other students in lab coats. I bet this is the group she meets with every week."

Lee was now searching the dresser drawers. "When are you going to talk to them?"

"Tomorrow," Katherine answered as she continued to flip through photos. The last one in the stack showed Olivia with her arm around a vivacious young woman with short brown hair and fair skin. "The inscription says, 'New Years Eve 2009 with Susan and Meg' The words 'not pictured' are in brackets under Meg's name. This is from just a couple weeks ago."

Lee stood and leaned against the dresser. "I found a notebook in her car with the name Meg Russell and a phone number. I sent it to Sammi."

"Great. Too bad Meg isn't in the photo, but at least we have a few more friends to talk with." Katherine pocketed the picture of Olivia and Susan and put the other photos back on top of the dresser where they were.

"Here's Olivia's passport." Lee held up the document. "She must not have been planning to leave the country."

"No sign of a suitcase anywhere. Her father said she has a blue suitcase with wheels."

"Looks to me like she packed a bag and went on a little trip." Lee returned everything to its place and closed the drawers.

Katherine lifted a shoulder. "I understand that's what the police officer thought when he checked in on Sunday. If that's what happened, Sammi should be able to find something online about her travel arrangements."

Katherine looked through the bathroom while Lee searched the small kitchen. A clear plastic organizer hung on the wall near the mirror. The two compartments on the top shelf held a hairdryer, a bottle of leave-in conditioner, and a dry shampoo spray. The lower shelf had many more compartments, almost empty except a few stray hair ties and cotton swabs. Katherine surmised the smaller compartments ordinarily held makeup and hair care products. An empty toothbrush holder on the sink seemed like a further sign that Olivia had packed her own suitcase.

"Nothing interesting in the kitchen." Lee called as he reentered the living area. "Nothing looks out of place, no signs of struggle or forced entry…other than ours." Lee laughed when Katherine made a face at his comment.

"I checked for scratches before I forced the door. There were none." She told Lee what she found in the bathroom.

"There was a bag full of all kinds of hairstyling tools and things in the back of her car. But no clothes or toothbrush. Nothing like that."

"It seems odd we didn't find any books or study notes. Wouldn't a grad student working on a research project need that kind of thing?"

"Maybe she took her study materials with her." Lee examined the nearly empty desktop.

Katherine wasn't convinced. She pursed her lips and stared out the window. It overlooked the alley behind the building. Olivia could have seen and heard if anyone was coming up to her apartment. She wouldn't have been surprised. And yet…

"I'm telling you, Lee, something is off about this room." Katherine couldn't shake the gnawing of her intuition. She did another visual sweep. She scanned the pictures lining the shelves. Then she realized what was missing.

"Lee, have you seen any pictures of Robert?"

"I don't think so, come to think of it. Mr. Ames said he's young, brown hair, blue eyes?"

"Yeah." They both looked more closely at the people in the photographs around the room. "It seems like she has framed photos of all the important people in her life."

"Here are pictures of Olivia with her mom and dad, a couple other girls..." Lee crouched to get a better look at the photos on lower shelves.

"Here's one of her with Dean Murphy and her father. But none of her young man. If she was enough in love with this guy to run away with him, why doesn't she have any pictures of him?"

"Good question. Maybe she took them with her?"

Katherine shook her head. "Why would she take a picture of him with her if she was going out with him Friday night? She didn't take everything; it looks like she planned to come back. And the unframed photos in her room. None showed a man answering Robert's description."

Lee crossed his arms. "If he's a con artist, he wouldn't want her to have his picture, would he? Sounds like we have more questions for this mystery man. Let's hope Jake finds him soon."

7

Jake turned in at Campus Security ten minutes after leaving the boxing gym. He was early for his meeting with Lee to help go through security footage. While he waited, Jake took the opportunity to interview the on-duty campus patrol officer.

"When my mum died last year, Olivia baked a delicious casserole and brought it to my home." The burly middle-aged officer's face lit up as he shared his story. "To be honest, most people don't bother to give us a second thought."

Jake could see the impact of Olivia's thoughtful gesture. "Sounds like Olivia is a good person."

"She's the real deal." Officer Ryan nodded. "Have you checked with Ames Enterprises security? They should know where Miss Ames is."

"They don't provide personal security for her," Jake said.

"Maybe not usually, but after the payroll fraud case blew up last year…" Ryan shook his head slowly. "They sent someone out here to check in on her."

"Did they?" Jake was surprised. He was sure Katherine had said Ames' security was not keeping tabs on Olivia. "Was he a tall young man with brown hair and blue eyes?"

Ryan laughed. "No, no. He was short and fat. About my age. Going bald. I can't remember his name, but he said he was working for Ames Enterprises."

"What did he want to know?"

"Her class schedule and what car she drives."

"Didn't it seem odd that someone who was working for Ames Enterprises would not know what kind of car Olivia Ames drives?" Jake raised an eyebrow.

Officer Ryan's mouth fell open. "Well, now you mention it. I didn't even think of that. Maybe he was new to the company?"

"Maybe. Did you give him what he wanted?"

"I don't have information about her class schedule. But yes. I did give him her car make, model, and license number."

When Lee got to Campus Security, he sensed tension between Jake and the officer at the desk. He introduced himself and asked if they were able to access the security video. When the officer stepped away, Jake told him about the odd older man asking questions about Olivia.

Another security officer came in and led them to a small room with three computers.

"All our security footage is stored digitally on these devices. We use 2-megapixel bullet cameras all over campus." He puffed out his chest. "We just upgraded four years ago."

Jake and Lee glanced at each other, neither willing to burst the man's bubble. Technology had advanced rapidly in the last four years. Two-megapixels wasn't the worst camera. But both former government agents had worked with much more sophisticated equipment. When the officer finished his explanation, he left them to go through the old footage.

"Whoa, this image must be 480 pixels." Lee gave a low whistle and feigned excitement.

Jake smirked. "At least it's better than all the grainy CCTV footage we had to wade through last week."

"Can't argue with you there." Lee turned one of the chairs around backwards to straddle it. He started pulling up digital files recorded when Olivia could have been on campus. He had analyzed thousands of hours of video files during his time as an analyst at the NSA. As a private detective, Lee's skills had just as much use, but with less of the bureaucratic red tape. Which suited him just fine.

Jake's phone beeped. "Looks like we've got a possible lead on Robert after all. My buddy in forensics just sent me a digital fingerprint file on the guy."

Lee looked up in surprise. "They've got his prints?"

"Apparently, several months ago, Ames brought them a glass liquor bottle in a plastic bag. He bullied them into lifting the prints, but they didn't match it to anything."

"Fingerprints off a glass bottle. Not too shabby. Wonder how he managed it?"

"He probably asked Robert to pour the drinks one night he was at his house," Jake mused.

"Can you send those prints to one of your contacts?"

"I have a friend in the FBI's Criminal Justice Information Services. Let me give them a call." Jake called his contact and filled him in on the story.

Lee squinted at the computer monitors in front of him, watching images fly by at double speed. Something caught his eye as he heard Jake ask his friend to run Robert's prints through the FBI's system.

Lee ran the footage back and slowed it to normal speed. "Are they going to run the prints?"

"Yeah." Jake said as he tapped at his iPhone 3G. "I just sent them the file."

Lee replayed the same section of footage, slower this time, and zoomed in on a section of the image. He asked, "When will we hear back?"

"Forty-eight hours. My contact owes me a couple favors."

"Well, I guess all we can do now is babysit this security footage." Lee pulled a big bag of Utz potato chips out of his backpack and grinned. "Good thing I brought snacks!"

"I'm looking for more information about a student, Robert Norton." Katherine sat in a chair facing Mary Yoseff's large desk. "He may know the whereabouts of a student who appears to be missing, Olivia Ames."

"Olivia missing? How dreadful." Ms. Yoseff pushed her reading glasses up into her dark hair, furrowing her brow in concern. "How can I help?"

"I'm hoping you have information in Robert Norton's admissions records that can help us locate him. An address, phone number, email...anything would help."

"When would you say Mr. Norton was admitted?" Ms. Yoseff picked up her desk phone and punched a few buttons.

"I really don't know. I understand he's been dating Olivia about a year."

"Oh! I know who you're talking about now!" Ms. Yoseff spoke to her assistant on the phone. "Find the records for Robert Norton. He would have registered last year, before the spring semester. Thanks." Ms. Yoseff hung up the phone and pushed back in her seat. "He's been to several student body functions with Olivia. It took me a minute to put a name to him."

"What can you tell me about them?"

"Well, Olivia is amazing. A lot of students struggle to find themselves at college, but not her! She's always known exactly what she wanted, ever since she was a grad student. She's laser focused on her career and passionate about bio-medical research." Ms. Yoseff beamed.

"Have you noticed changes in Olivia's behavior recently? Or in the last year or so since she met Robert?"

"Well, there was one unusual thing last fall. I had a meeting scheduled with her to talk about career planning. She canceled because she said she was still considering her options. That was odd. She's always been so sure about what she wanted to do with her life. But I didn't really think much of it at the time."

"Did she reschedule the meeting?"

"No. She didn't." Ms. Yoseff pursed her lips.

"And what about Robert?" Out of the corner of her eye, Katherine noticed someone standing outside the office door, which stood slightly ajar.

"I don't know that much about him. I believe he was enrolling in the engineering program, although he asked about classes in several degree programs. He mentioned bio-med specifically and asked if he could meet some of the professors and students."

"Is that unusual?" Katherine asked.

"No. Most kids don't know what they want to do until they've explored their options. Of course, Robert was a little older than most undergrads, but he had just left the Navy."

Katherine looked around the room and saw the figure still standing at the crack in the door. He was a slim man with shaggy red hair and a fair complexion who appeared to be in his late twenties. This time he realized he'd been noticed. He knocked lightly and stepped into the room.

"Excuse me. I just need to drop off this application," he said, holding out a thick blue folio.

"Gordon, maybe you can help us. Ms. Carson here is asking about Robert Norton."

Gordon scratched the coarse stubble on his chin. "What about him?"

Katherine stood to face the young man, who was a good six inches taller than she was. "Do you know Robert well?"

Gordon scoffed. "No. He's not in graduate school. Met him once or twice when Olivia brought him to our lab group. But he wasn't interested in bio-medical research. He only wanted to talk about Olivia."

Ms. Yoseff grabbed her phone when it rang.

"You mean Olivia Ames, right?" Katherine heard a trace of derision in Gordon's voice.

Gordon put his hands in his pockets. "Yeah, Olivia and I are in the same program of study."

"What kinds of questions did Robert ask about her?"

"Oh, her personality, what kind of research partner she was. Things like that. Seemed to me he was hunting for a smart chick to hook up with from day one. And he headed straight for Olivia. She was the smartest one of all."

"I'm afraid I have some disturbing information." Ms. Yoseff's tone was crisp. She cleared her throat. "There are no records on Robert Norton."

"What does that mean?" Katherine had a sinking feeling that she knew.

"It means he never registered. In any degree program."

8

Katherine lowered herself back into the chair facing the desk. If the man they knew as Robert was not registered, the implication was jarring. "Could he have registered earlier?"

"We started computerizing our enrollment records nine years ago. He isn't in the system." Ms. Yoseff looked upset. "Do you think this man came on campus to make trouble?"

"Worse. He may have been targeting Olivia, given what Gordon said." Katherine turned in her chair to look for the young man, but he was gone.

"Gordon isn't the most personable of our students. I apologize." Ms. Yoseff pushed her glasses back into her hair.

"Dean Murphy mentioned there was some competition between Olivia and Gordon?"

"There shouldn't be, but as I said, Gordon's communication skills leave something to be desired. I could see the two of them butting heads over a project component."

"Well, I'll have to find time to talk to him again."

Ms. Yoseff wrung her hands. "What should I do about Robert? If he isn't registered as a student, he has no business being on campus as much as he is."

"Call the police." Katherine grabbed a pen and pad of sticky notes from the Dean's desk and jotted down a phone number. "Contact Detective Camilla Alvarez, Baltimore PD Missing Persons. This might be the suspicious circumstances they need to open an official police investigation into Olivia's whereabouts." She handed over the note with Detective Alvarez's name and phone number.

"I will. I'll do it right away." Ms. Yoseff had the phone in her hand the moment Katherine stepped out of the office.

Sammi had spent hours talking to local travel agents. But, she hadn't gotten any information. She stared at the sticky note on her desk. Lee had asked her to research Meg Russell and the phone number he found in Olivia's car. A quick internet search didn't give her any results. Usually she did basic information gathering, taking messages, and online research. She wasn't supposed to have contact with suspects.

But no one said anything about this Meg being a suspect ... she'd probably be happy to help. Better still, maybe Olivia is at Meg's place right now and this whole farce can be over with in just a few minutes...

"Hello, I'm calling for Meg Russell."

"That's me." The woman on the other end of the phone call sounded older than she'd expected, and a little gruff.

"Hi, my name is Sammi Garcia. I'm calling about a friend of yours, Olivia Ames?"

"What about her?"

"I work for a private detective—"

"Private detective! How did you get this number?"

"Olivia had it written down. We're trying to locate her." Sammi chewed her lip. She wasn't supposed to give out information about active cases.

"Well, I don't know where she is."

"Okay, can you tell me how you know Olivia? When was the last time you saw her?"

"I don't know her very well. We just met for the first time a couple weeks ago."

"Oh, that's interesting. And then she wrote down your phone number."

"Yeah, well we planned to keep in touch." Megan couldn't hide the defensive tone in her voice.

"But you haven't heard from her since then? What day did you say you saw her?"

"Look, how do I know you are who you say you are? I don't think I should be talking to you over the phone."

"Well if you give me your address, I can have one of our detectives come by and—"

"I don't think so. There's nothing I can tell you. I don't want to be involved."

The phone went dead. Sammi typed out a transcript of the strange conversation. Frustrated, she decided to crank up some music. Then she went to try to find Meg Russell on social media. She was just starting to search when she heard the outer door open. A minute later, Katherine stepped into the office. Sammi chuckled as her boss danced over to the sound system.

"Sorry, Chica," she said, turning the volume down. "Don't want our neighbors to complain. It's nearly time to go home anyway."

"Right, right. I had to put on something to keep my mind occupied."

"Slow going?" Katherine dropped into the chair at the other desk and relaxed.

Sammi rolled her eyes. "Her Myspace posts are all selfies and book recommendations."

"How about her search history? Any travel plans? Pictures of engagement rings or wedding traditions?"

"None that I know." Sammi scrunched down in her chair and started typing faster.

"Sammi? Did you check Olivia's search history?"

The deflection hadn't worked. "No, I haven't had time. I've been focusing on her social media and calling local travel agents to see if she had reservations."

"Samantha, I need you to check Olivia's search history, her sent emails, everything you can get a hold of. We need leads to follow." Katherine walked to the coffee table where Sammi had left Olivia's laptop and picked up the case.

Sammi protested. "I'm not comfortable with this. It's an invasion of privacy."

"It is part of our job. You came to me wanting to become a detective. You don't get to pick and choose which tasks you want to do." Katherine handed her the laptop case again.

"I might have found something out my way." Even to her own ears, the excuse sounded weak.

"But you didn't, or you would have already told me about it. Now you've wasted a whole day on a task that could have been done much more efficiently after you searched her computer."

Sammi let her defensiveness take over. "I didn't waste the day. I looked up her social media. I spoke with five different travel agencies on the phone. None of them would give me any information. I even called Meg Russell to…" Sammi bit her lip.

"You called a possible suspect?"

"Well…Lee didn't say she was a suspect." Sammi pouted.

"What did she say?"

"She said she didn't know where Olivia is."

"How does she know Olivia?"

"She wouldn't say."

Katherine ran her hands through her hair. "When did she last see her?"

"I don't know, she didn't want to talk to me."

"How did she know that Olivia was missing?"

"She didn't, until I told her."

"You told her? Samantha, you cannot give out that kind of information." Katherine put her hand to her forehead.

"I know, I know, but I wanted to help."

"I gave you a job to do, Sammi. You need to leave the investigating to the investigators. What if this Meg knows something?"

"I just didn't feel comfortable hacking into Olivia's computer until we know more about what is going on." Sammi wanted to defend her perspective.

"I'm not asking you to hack in, we have her passwords. She may very well have given them to her father in case something happened to her." Katherine tapped her palm with the back of her other hand to emphasize her words.

"You don't know that." Sammi did not want to back down. "And why did her father have her personal laptop anyway?"

"Her father took it to a computer repair shop in Wilmington last week at her request. He planned to return it this weekend when she visited. But he didn't get that chance."

Katherine took a deep breath. "If we lived in a perfect world, we would never need to pry into other people's business. In a perfect world, there would be no need for detectives of any kind. But this world is far from perfect. And there are times when we do need detectives. We have been hired to find this woman. If this is really what you want to do with your life, you are going to have to get used to a certain amount of prying and spying."

Sammi didn't answer. She couldn't win this argument. She put on her coat, picked up her bag, and grabbed Olivia's laptop. Then she headed out the door.

Katherine sat down at her desk with a groan as Sammi stormed out of the office. This wasn't the first time Sammi had walked out after they crossed a perceived line. It was getting on Katherine's nerves.

Sammi's aggravated exit reminded her of the gossip about Olivia and Robert's fight. Several people told her about the couple's Friday afternoon argument in the cafeteria. They exchanged heated words, and Olivia stormed off. It was the last time many people saw her.

Katherine typed her daily report on her computer. In the days before she went missing, Olivia had attended her usual classes and study groups.

Olivia's professors knew nothing about Robert or about her disappearance. They all agreed with Dean Murphy and called Olivia a bright and responsible young woman who would never run off without telling someone. Olivia's thesis advisor, Dr. Mahoney, had not been available, but Katherine scheduled a meeting with him for the morning.

She got the story about the fight from students who shared classes with Olivia. Everyone knew who her father was, even though she was discreet. That made her life fodder for the rumor mill.

Katherine was typing her final thoughts into the report when Lee and Jake walked in. "Hey, guys, any luck?"

Jake hung up his coat and summarized his morning interviews. "We haven't been able to get a clear picture of Robert from any of the video we've reviewed so far. I think I'll drive up to Wilmington tomorrow and get Mr. Ames to help me with a sketch. But Lee did spot something interesting on the security footage."

Lee took the cue to pull out his phone and show Katherine some still shots he'd taken of the video. "A short, balding guy sitting in the quad on December 31. Sitting outside reading a newspaper in the middle of a Maryland winter?" Lee made a face and pulled his scarf tighter.

Katherine chuckled and peered at the screen as Lee swiped through the stills.

Lee continued, "This same figure shows up several times over the course of at least three days. Always strange places. Always within sight of Olivia."

Jake said, "And he matches the description of someone who was asking questions about Olivia at campus security. The man pretended to be working for Ames Enterprises."

Katherine took the phone from Lee and zoomed in on one of the shots that captured part of the man's face. Her lips parted. "I know who this is."

Jake stepped behind her to look over her shoulder.

"That's Martin Lansing."

"Who?" Both men asked.

"He goes by 'Marty Slye.' He has a whole schtick." Katherine rolled her eyes. "I tripped over him last year when you guys were in Ft. Mead. He's probably the most incompetent private detective to ever darken the door of city hall. But he's cheap, so he's popular."

"Let me guess, you gave him the benefit of the doubt and got burned for it?" Jake tutted.

"Doesn't he have a billboard over in Curtis Bay?" Lee asked.

"That's him. I did try to work with him until I caught him planting evidence. Then I warned him that if he ever meddled in one of my cases again, I'd do more than report him to the licensing board."

Lee snickered. "What on earth is he doing trailing Olivia?"

Katherine wrinkled her nose. "I would certainly like to know the answer."

"You want me to track him down?" Jake asked.

"Actually, I'm pretty sure I know exactly where he'll be." Katherine looked at her watch. "You two get your dailies written. I want to handle Marty myself."

9

When Katherine entered the dingy diner, the bell above the door jingled. The place smelled of burnt toast and smoke. She spotted Marty at a corner booth, hunched over a plate of greasy fries. His eyes went wide when he saw her and a clump of fries fell onto his paunch. Without a second thought, he wrenched himself from the booth, knocking over his plate.

"Hey!" Katherine shouted over the commotion as Marty's plate hit the floor. She didn't expect him to be happy to see her, but why would he run? She pushed her way around nosy patrons and a disgruntled server, crossing the room toward the back door where Marty fled.

The door led to a narrow alley behind the diner. Marty was halfway up the block, but Kathcrine's long legs ate up the ground between them. Marty glanced back and pushed himself harder to stay out of reach, his short legs churning like pistons. He swerved around the corner and crashed through a garbage can and a large pile of trash.

Katherine dodged soda cans and crumpled paper, never letting her target get out of sight. She was vaguely impressed with how fast the little man could run.

Marty and Katherine exploded onto the busy street. Steam

rose from the manhole covers and drain grates as they zig-zagged through rush hour traffic. Marty smacked into the side of gray sedan and the driver blared his horn. Katherine used the distraction to veer between two vehicles and gain ground.

The odor of exhaust fumes hung in the air as they dodged and spun to avoid more collisions. Marty's eyes peered anxiously over his shoulder. Katherine kept pace only feet behind him. Her steady breathing contrasted with the loud car horns and engines around them.

Marty's sneakers squealed as he swerved off the street into an abandoned construction site. If he hoped to lose Katherine in the sea of yellow tape, he'd made a miscalculation. Her footfalls remained measured and rhythmic, as if she'd navigated this obstacle course before. Marty slipped and cursed quietly, his frustration echoing off the metal beams.

Katherine slowed down as she closed the final feet between them. Her target was cornered. Marty attempted a final desperate move, grabbing some scaffolding to haul himself up. The cold metal groaned in protest and shook under his weight. Katherine reacted instinctively as the scaffolding began to shudder. She leapt over the scattered debris, snatched Marty by his belt, and pulled with all her strength. She managed to rip Marty away mere moments before the neglected structure toppled over, sending a billow of dust and debris into the air.

They both covered their faces and waited for the dust to settle. Marty's chest heaved as he gaped at the place where he had been standing moments before.

He coughed and stammered. "You saved me."

"Don't get sentimental on me, Marty, I need information." Her eyes blazed with intensity. "Why did you run?"

"Are you kidding? The last thing I want is to tangle with you again. I couldn't believe it when they told me you'd be on the other side of the case." Marty tried to scramble to his feet.

"What case? And who's they?" Katherine helped Marty up.

"The prosecutors. The stolen pesticide?"

"Marty, I don't know what you're talking about. I haven't heard about stolen pesticide. I'm here to ask for your help," Katherine gritted her teeth, "as one professional to another."

"Oh." Marty looked relieved and straightened his coat. "In that case, sure. Anything you want."

"Great. I'm looking for a young woman who has gone missing. Tell me why you were following Olivia Ames."

The color drained from his face and he leaned against the wall. "I don't know what you're talking about!"

"Don't lie to me, Marty," Katherine snapped. She leaned in close. "I saw you on campus security footage."

Marty wiped his face with a meaty hand. "I was hired to tail her, that's all. Some guy with a fat wallet slipped me a wad of cash and told me to track her daily routine."

"Who was he?" Katherine pressed, taking a step closer.

"I don't know his name," Marty whined. "I figured it was just another jealous boyfriend or snooping spouse. I had no idea she'd go missing."

"You might have played a role in her disappearance, Marty."

"Come on, Kat, I'm trying to help you!"

Katherine slapped her hand against the wall behind him, inches from his head. "Only friends call me Kat." She lowered her face to line up with his and spoke in a low, menacing voice. "And you've never helped anyone but yourself in your whole life."

Marty's eyes darted from side to side, avoiding her piercing stare. "He was just some guy in a suit, like a million others you see every day. He used one of those cheap, pre-paid phones you can buy at any convenience store."

"You're telling me that you didn't immediately recognize the daughter of one of the richest men on the east coast? Don't make me laugh, Marty."

Marty shifted uncomfortably. "Yeah, I did recognize her. I suggested that such a high-profile case might be worth more money. But he didn't go for it."

"And you just accepted that?" Katherine glowered.

Marty shook his head. "He said if I didn't want the case, he'd give it to someone back in Wilmington, but they wanted someone local for convenience."

"Back in Wilmington?"

"That's what he said. And he said 'they' could get someone else. I figured it had something to do with Ames Enterprises and…" He rubbed his neck.

"And you didn't think it was suspicious that someone from Ames Enterprises would want to hire you, of all the detectives in the city?" Katherine pressed her lips together.

Marty puffed out his chest and started to protest, but his bravado melted in the face of Katherine's stare. "Of course it was weird, but I'm not in the business of investigating anything that doesn't pay. And once I turn in the final report, it's none of my business what the client does with it."

Katherine leaned back to give the man more breathing room now that he was starting to tell the truth. She knew from previous encounters that Marty might figuratively pull the rug out from under his own grandmother to make a buck. But she didn't believe he would be in on a kidnapping.

"Tell me everything, when you met, what he asked for, what he looks like. Any detail could be important."

Marty's head bobbed up and down. He gestured wildly as he described the man who had approached him in the middle of December. "Over six feet tall, skinny, white with brown eyes, no distinguishing marks. His coat was open and he had on a dark suit, no tie. I couldn't tell his hair color since he was clean shaved and had on earmuffs and a hat. He wanted to know everything about Olivia's movements, her habits, and her schedule. Who she spent time with and what she did with her time off."

Katherine's brow furrowed. "The holidays are a bad time to be learning about people's habits. Why would he want you to follow her then?"

"I don't know, Kat—Katherine. I honestly don't. The guy handed me two grand to follow her, and he promised me two more after I turned in my report. Which I delivered last week, and he paid me again in cash."

"Was anything off about the money?"

Marty smirked. "I know phony money and this wasn't. All good, crisp, clean hundred-dollar bills, fresh from the bank."

"That's interesting."

"You think so?" Marty shrugged. "Like you said, not much was going. I sat on the girl's apartment mostly. She went to the library several days. She works there. She met with a couple teachers, some friends. Talked on the phone with her dad a lot."

"You listened in on her phone calls? How?"

Marty shifted uncomfortably. "Don't get your panties in a wad, I just used a standard parabolic mic."

Katherine glared.

"I know, I know. I mean, I didn't bug the kid's apartment or anything, I just listened in when she was on the phone and talking to people. SOP."

Illegal, Katherine thought. But she was intrigued. "Did she have any interesting conversations?"

"None. Seems like she has a couple lady friends, a boyfriend, and, like I said, she talks to her dad every day."

"Did you get a look at her boyfriend? Was he the man who hired you?"

"No way." Marty waved his hands. "I got a good look at him. He caught me taking some pictures and warned me off. I told him I was a reporter, which he seemed to buy. There's no way the boyfriend is my client."

"And was it you asking questions about Olivia at campus security?"

Marty pulled at his collar. "Yeah, that was me. I figured they'd cough up more if they thought I was from Ames Enterprises."

Katherine studied the smarmy detective for a moment, assessing the truth of his words. Finally, she nodded, satisfied. "Okay, Marty." She handed him a business card. "Send me all your notes. Everything you have."

"Absolutely." Marty said. "And then...?"

"Then I won't tell the police about your illegal use of a listening device."

Marty gulped and stuffed her card into his pocket. "Right."

"Get out of here, Marty. If I find out you're lying, I'll be back."

Marty stumbled across the rubble. Katherine watched his frantic exit with a steady gaze. She knew she couldn't trust the man, but she didn't think he was lying either. Not this time. A tall, thin man in a suit, whose identity and motives are unclear. If Marty's client wasn't Robert, could he be connected to him? Or did Olivia catch the attention of an entirely different person? Maybe, for entirely different reasons.

10

"I just can't get through to her." Katherine had just finished recounting her argument with Sammi. She squeezed an extra wedge of lime into her strawberry limeade.

"She'll come around. At least you take the time to try to guide her instead of turning her out on her ear."

Katherine's companion was a petite woman with porcelain skin and short black curls. She was dressed immaculately in a blazer and red blouse. She looked every inch the powerhouse lawyer. Margaret Mitchell had been Katherine's friend since they were little girls. They'd been meeting for dinner regularly ever since Katherine moved back to Baltimore.

"Thanks, Mags. I just hate to be the one to knock the sparkle out of her eyes."

Margaret poured more steaming hot tea into her cup and added another packet of sugar. "Somebody has to, hon. Better it's someone who cares about her than someone who could take advantage of her."

Katherine stared into her half-empty glass and listened to the clink and clatter of the bar area. She supposed Margaret was right. *Every girl has to grow up eventually. I wonder if Olivia has grown up?* Katherine had found a knight in shining armor to marry by the time she was Olivia's age. She recalled being young and in love. Reckless. Daring. Vulnerable. Daniel would never take advantage of her. He only ever protected her.

The Espionage Services Agency had brought the two of them together. They worked together on many missions, their talents balancing and enhancing one another. But the Agency didn't foresee that Daniel and Katherine would fall in love. And ESA didn't approve when they got married. She often wondered how their lives would be different if they hadn't taken that step.

"Katherine?" Margaret placed her hand on her friend's arm to pull her back to the present.

Katherine put down her glass and stretched out the hand that had it in a death grip. "Sorry, Mags."

"You were thinking about him weren't you?"

Katherine didn't answer. She didn't have to. Margaret knew who haunted her reveries.

"Anyway, I want you to know you're doing a great job with Sammi. I'm so glad you were willing to take her on last year. She was by far the best student in my class."

"Thanks, Mags." Katherine grinned, happy to shake off memories of lost love. "I'm glad you brought her to me. She is going to become a great detective someday. She's got instinct, intuition, and integrity."

"A triple threat!" Margaret smiled and leaned forward. "Reminds me of someone else I know."

Katherine smirked. "My instinct and intuition tell me there's a request behind that compliment."

"And your integrity will tell you to take this case." Margaret pulled a file out of her bag and slid it across the table.

Katherine leaned back in her chair and picked up the folder.

"I suppose this will be a pro bono case then?"

Margaret raised her shoulders to her ears and grinned. "I'll buy your dinner!"

Katherine grinned at her friend's shameless ingratiation. She remembered fondly the first time Mags had sweet-talked her into investigating a case. After an early morning stakeout, the girls learned that no one was overfeeding the goldfish. Mags' daddy had bought a new, chubby goldfish to replace the one that had died. The girls never told Mr. Mitchell they'd found out, and the Mitchells kept replacing dead goldfish until Mags started high school. These days the mysteries were much more serious.

"Okay, Mags, okay. What do you want us to do?"

"My client has been charged with stealing a large quantity of pesticide."

Flipping through the file, Katherine made an unpleasant face. "Twenty-five kilograms of chlorpyrifos? Nasty stuff."

"You've heard of it?"

Katherine nodded. "If ingested, a twenty-milligram dose is more than enough to be lethal."

"I won't ask why you know that. My client says she has an alibi for the time of the theft."

Katherine paused as a waitress brought her another strawberry limeade. "This must be the case Marty Slye was worried about."

"How did you know about him?"

"I had a conference of sorts with him about another case. But he mentioned something about stolen pesticide, and that he's on the prosecutor's side."

"He's one of their main witnesses. My client hired him to follow her husband, who was cheating on her. Marty is going to testify about what he found out. That her husband planned to take their savings and run away. I'm sure the prosecution will use that as motive."

Katherine shrugged. "Sounds more like a motive for murder than theft. Why do the police think she's guilty?"

Margaret emptied her teacup and started browsing the menu. "I think she's just the most convenient suspect. And I must admit her alibi is a bit far-fetched."

"Your table is ready, ladies." The hostess escorted them to a booth near a large window. The aroma of fresh bread and garlic filled the air. A waiter swooped in to take their order.

Margaret continued, "At the time of the theft, my client was supposed to be picking up supplies at a distributor in Wilmington. She had the wrong address and wandered around for nearly an hour trying to find the building."

"That's the hole in her alibi that the police can't see past."

"Yep. It was late at night so no one can corroborate her story. Except…" Margaret patted the table to provide her own drumroll. "She stopped to ask directions from a man taking a break outside a building construction site. He gave her a cigarette and they chatted a couple minutes before she left. She's pretty sure he'll remember her."

"So you want us to find your witness."

Margaret flashed her best "Yes, please, and thank you" grin. A waiter placed a bowl of spinach and artichoke dip and a basket of French bread in the center of the table.

"Okay, Mags. I'll send Jake up to look for your witness."

After dinner, Katherine drove to her apartment building on Knollwood Road. She parked under a street lamp, turned off her car, and relaxed into the seat. The glow of the old street lamp allowed her to see a few feet in all directions before fading to darkness. Katherine groaned, searching for the motivation to go inside. Her mixed emotions reflected the muddle of the Ames' case. The chilly silence was broken by the ring of her BlackBerry. She answered on the second ring.

"Hey, Katie."

"Hi, Jake." Katherine unbuckled her seatbelt and straightened up in her seat.

"Did you make it inside your apartment?"

Katherine slumped back. "You always know, don't you?"

"You okay? Seems like this case is getting to you."

"I guess so. I wanted this to be easy money...find a run-away heiress, let the family figure out the relationship mess." Katherine got out of her car and climbed the steps to her apartment.

"I suppose nothing is ever that simple."

"I suppose not." Katherine unlocked her apartment door and stepped into the nearly bare living room. "I just wish we had more to go on. The clues we do have seem to conflict with each other. And I think Sammi is on strike."

"Again?" Jake chuckled.

Katherine huffed as she removed her coat and bolted the door. "What does she think detectives do? We can't find missing people by looking into a crystal ball." Katherine lowered herself onto the soft couch, the only piece of furniture in the room.

"Even if we could, she'd probably think that was spying, too." Jake chuckled louder. "Cut her some slack, Katie. We were all young and naive once."

Jake knew better than most people exactly how young and

naive Katherine had once been. He was the closest thing to family she had.

"Anyway, I'd like to believe Olivia wouldn't run off ..."

Jake finished her thought. "But it's possible that this Robert character manipulated her into doing something she would not normally do."

"If that's the case, then I want to find Olivia before she does something she'll regret. I hope it's not too late." Katherine bit her lower lip and shifted into manager mode. "You said you were going up to Wilmington tomorrow?"

"Right. I want to get Mr. Ames to help with a sketch of Robert."

"After you're finished with Ames, I need you to do some digging. Find what construction companies worked on the evening of January 8th."

"In this weather?"

"That's the story. Margaret asked for our help finding a witness to corroborate a client's alibi." She filled Jake in on the details. "See if you can locate this man, take his statement, and, assuming it backs up her story, get it to Margaret."

"Sounds like a plan. Let me know if you find out any more information from Maggie's client." Jake ended the call, leaving Katherine to think about the conversation. She secretly hoped her two best friends would end up together someday. She just had a feeling—and Jake was the only person on earth who could get away with calling the lawyer "Maggie."

She got up from the couch and picked up a well-worn copy of *The Wonderful Wizard of Oz* from the stack of books in the corner. She would either fall asleep reading or stay up until the wee hours to finish it. In either case, her mind would have an escape from the worries of the day.

11

Jake got up early to start the ninety-minute drive to Wilmington. He climbed in his Jeep and turned on his iPhone's Bluetooth. He'd resisted many technological advancements for a long time. But once Sammi showed him how to use his phone's Bluetooth, he never looked back. Being able to make calls during his drive time greatly increased his productivity. He loved anything that could make him more efficient.

Last night, Katherine had dropped a new assignment in his lap. Jake called information services in Wilmington to get phone numbers for construction contractors in the area. Then he started calling them to find out who had a crew working on January 8th on the east side of town. Fortunately, the middle of winter isn't the most popular time for construction projects. He only had to call two companies to find his lead.

As soon as he parked in the Ames Enterprises parking lot, he sent an email to the safety manager at Webber Construction asking for information about who was on the site that day.

Then he grabbed his backpack with his sketch materials and walked toward the tall, modern building.

Katherine had asked him to try to figure out who besides Robert might be following Olivia. Without telling the already distressed father about that new bit of information. Not yet.

Jake entered the large glass doors and approached the front desk. A security guard directed him to Mr. Ames' office.

Jake handed his card to the executive's assistant who hurried into the inner office. The woman returned a moment later, followed by Mr. Ames.

Jake extended his hand. "Jake Mercer. I work for Carson Investigations. I believe Katherine told you I was coming."

"Yes, of course. Please come in."

As he entered the spacious office, Jake noticed a large framed photograph on a table by the wall. It stood out because of its size and because, unlike the nearby smaller photos of Olivia and her father, it showed a group of six people. A younger version of Jonathan Ames stood with his arm around a young woman holding a baby. On his other side, a blonde woman stood with her hands on the shoulders of two children, a boy, about 12, and a girl, about 8.

"Is this your family?" Jake asked.

"It was. My wife and my sister both died years ago. All I have left is Olivia."

"The other children?"

"My sister's children. She raised them on her own, gave them our last name. But I'm not sure even she knew who the fathers were."

"Where are they now?"

"I honestly couldn't tell you, detective. My sister was an actress. Her stage name was Linda Bailey. Our father left us each half of a sizable estate. I invested the money and built this company. Linda spent her half on costumes and musical productions and lovers. When she ran out of money, she and the children lived with us for a while. Then Olivia was born, and I set them up in a little house outside Philadelphia. Arranged for her to get a job. But that wasn't enough for her. She sold the house, packed up her kids, and headed back to New York. I never heard from her again. The last I heard of her was when her son Victor called to tell me she had died."

"I'm sorry for your loss."

Mr. Ames shrugged. "I'd lost Linda long before that. And Victor only called to try to get money out of me. Seemed to think he should be entitled to my money since he was my nephew. I told him that his mother had spent his inheritance, and that was that."

"And the girl?"

"I think she lives in a city close to Baltimore now. She's all right, at least she would be if she stayed away from that brother of hers. She sent her condolences when Della died. And I sent her a wedding gift when she got married. I hope you've not come here just to ask about my estranged family. The only thing I care about right now is Olivia."

"Of course. My associates are looking for leads to follow as we speak."

"What can I do to help? I assume it's too soon to expect any results?"

Jake sighed. "Unfortunately, these things take time."

Mr. Ames nodded solemnly. He couldn't hide the disappointment in his eyes.

"We've been focusing on Robert's possible connection to your daughter's absence. And we will find out the extent of his involvement, believe me. But I wonder if there might be someone else we should consider. Perhaps a rival, an ex-employee, or other enemy who would want to see you hurt?"

"I can't think of anyone."

Jake pressed. "A man in your position is bound to have enemies. Your company is worth millions. I understand you just discovered some rather severe losses last year, for example."

Mr. Ames furrowed his brow and straightened up in his chair. "Yes. An internal audit found several fake employees. They had been getting paid for the last five or six years. I'm not an accountant, but I understand we lost hundreds of thousands of dollars to this salary padding scheme"

"Have the culprits been identified?"

Mr. Ames shook his head. "I think they're narrowing it down. I was under suspicion myself last fall, but the task force cleared me and moved on to other suspects. My security and accounting departments have focused on nothing else since the fraud was discovered. But since many of the identities were completely fictitious, they're having trouble pinning the crime to the real person behind it."

Jake sighed. "I don't suppose there is a way that incident could have anything to do with Olivia's disappearance?"

"I can't see how it would. Olivia isn't involved in my business. But I can have our CFO get you copies of our records. Anything we can give you. Of course, some files are in the possession of the FBI and IRS investigators."

"My associate Lee has experience in forensic accounting. I'll tell him to get in contact with your CFO. But back to the subject of Robert, there is something you can do to help us. We need a picture to help us locate him."

"I don't have a picture of Robert."

"I know," Jake smiled reassuringly. "That's why I brought this." He pulled a sketchbook, pencils, and eraser putty out of the bag he'd been carrying. "Let's get to work."

Katherine was at the office early as usual, prepping for the day ahead. She had an morning appointment with Olivia's thesis advisor, followed by a visit to the open lab she'd been hearing so much about. Her thoughts were interrupted when the office door opened.

"Good morning, Sammi." Katherine tried to make eye contact with the younger woman. "How are you?"

Sammi stood silent a moment longer, then looked up to meet Katherine's gaze. "I apologize for last night. For being disrespectful. Insolent."

Katherine suspected that Sammi's aunt and uncle had sided with the boss. "It's okay, Samantha. I may have been too hard on you, too."

Sammi pulled Olivia's laptop out of her backpack. "I'm still not very comfortable prying into someone's private life. But I know I can't choose what tasks I'm assigned. I'm ready to do better today."

Sammi put the laptop on the coffee table. When the profile loaded, the screen filled with a close-up picture of Olivia and her father. "Seems like Olivia really is close to her dad. And you were right about checking her computer sooner; it would have given us more leads."

"You found something already?" Katherine sat on the sofa next to her assistant.

"Yeah. I checked her search history last night. It's full of info on bio-printing, organ donations, organ transplants, and transplant surgeons. But nothing on wedding or vacation plans. She hadn't even been researching weekend getaways, much less booking hotel reservations. I found a more recent picture of her on Facebook." Sammi tapped a few keys and a photo of a blonde with short curly hair popped on screen.

Katherine hummed. "Well, that's a change."

To the right of the photo was a short block of text, "Starting 2009 with a new hairdo!"

"I wonder why Mr. Ames didn't mention to me she'd changed her hairstyle."

"He probably didn't know." Sammi tapped a few more keys and pointed to her screen. "Olivia still has a public Myspace page that has an older photo, with long brown hair. From what I can tell, this is the page that her father can see online. The new hairstyle post is on Facebook, and it looks like Mr. Ames hasn't made the switch."

"Is it normal to have two social media accounts?"

Sammi shot her a sympathetic look. "Yes. Not uncommon at all. And her Facebook account is less than a year old, so it probably doesn't mean anything that her father is not her friend."

Katherine ignored the social media jargon. "Ms. Nichols told Lee about Olivia's hair appointment, but didn't know the stylist. Is there a way to tell when and where this picture was taken?"

"Yes, the picture was posted at 4:07 PM on Friday. And she tagged the Cut Right Salon—that must be where she got her hair styled. I found something else interesting on Facebook."

Sammi grinned as she opened Olivia's friend list and pointed to one of the names.

Katherine read it aloud. "Victor B. Ames. That's Jonathan Ames' nephew!"

"Didn't Mr. Ames say they weren't on speaking terms with his family?"

Katherine nodded. "Yes, he did. Maybe Olivia didn't feel as strongly about it."

"The other thing I noticed is that Victor has liked every single post that Olivia has put on her page. And she posts several times a day, every day."

"What does that mean?"

"It could mean they are very close, or that he's trying to get her attention. It's not normal for someone to like every post. It's also out of the ordinary for someone who posts every day like Olivia to suddenly go dark. But there hasn't been any activity on her social media since Friday. Oh, and there isn't a Robert or Bob on either of her friends lists."

Katherine listened intently to the information from her young assistant. "Robert is clearly keeping himself a secret. See if you can find addresses on the cousin and the hair salon."

Sammi carried the laptop to her desk and powered on her desktop computer. "I will get on that right away. I also looked up the names you and Lee found yesterday in Olivia's apartment."

"Did you find out who they are?"

"Not yet. But I did find Susan Campbell and Megan A. Russell on Olivia's Facebook friends list. I'll look into both of them more this afternoon."

"You did all this last night?" Katherine was impressed by Sammi's hard work. She recalled one of the few lessons from her mother: "People will rise to meet your expectations."

Sammi spoke softly. "I wanted to try to make up for the mistakes I made yesterday."

"Good work, Sammi. Let me know when you find those addresses. I want to check out the salon this afternoon. And I want you to come with me."

"Really?" Sammi bit back an excited smile.

Katherine walked to Sammi's desk. "Yes. You found this clue, it's only fair you get to help follow it up."

Sammi jumped up, squealed, and threw her arms around Katherine's neck. Then she quickly stepped back and bit her lip. She straightened her vest, trying to look professional despite the tears welling up in her eyes. "Gracias."

12

Lee sat at his desk in his home office, surrounded by monitors. The whirring fans and glowing screens made him feel at home, secure in the knowledge that the world was at his fingertips.

His eyes darted between screens as he skimmed two spread-sheets side by side. The files had been provided by Ames Enterprises and Lee was looking for patterns. The man who hired Marty had claimed a connection to the company. But none of the real employees stood out as potential suspects. That left the perpetrators of the salary padding fraud.

Lee's laptop chimed, indicating the start of a conference call. He clicked to join. Soon, Janet Springfield, the CFO of Ames Enterprises, and an FBI agent appeared on his screen.

"Lee, thanks for joining us," Janet said. "This is Ted Davis, lead investigator."

"Happy to help," Lee replied, adjusting his headset. "Let's dive in. I've already started analyzing the files you sent."

Ted tapped a pen on his notebook. "Great. We could use your expertise on this case. We've been cross-referencing with our own databases. So far, the false identities have been difficult to trace back to a single source."

Lee's fingers hovered over his keyboard. "Tell me more about the anomalies you've found."

Janet spent several minutes detailing their inquiry. They had flagged hundreds of payroll records as potentially suspicious. "These employees have similar hire dates, above-average salaries, and/or no direct supervisors."

"Interesting," Lee mused, scrolling through the entries. "And you've investigated all these addresses and contact details?"

"Yes," Ted confirmed. "Every single one has turned out to be a dead end."

Lee stared at the data. "Have you traced the bank accounts?"

Janet shook her head. "Most of the accounts were closed shortly after significant deposits. And they've layered multiple accounts from multiple banks. Whoever is behind this is covering their tracks well."

"There's always a trail," Lee said confidently. "What about the payments—were they all made from the same company account?"

Janet nodded. "Yes, they were."

Lee stretched his neck. "That suggests someone with significant access. Have you audited who has access to this account?"

Janet sighed. "We've tried, but it's a large company. Many people have access at different levels."

"So far, our investigation has focused on ruling out the most obvious suspects. Jonathan Ames, Ms. Springfield here, and the other executives." Ted jerked his thumb toward Janet.

Lee thought for a moment. "What about IT logs? Any unusual login patterns or access during odd hours?"

Ted leaned closer to the camera. "That's something we haven't fully explored."

Janet flipped through a folder. "Our IT department has logs, but we haven't analyzed them yet."

Lee let a smile tug at the corner of his mouth. "That's where we'll find our clue. We can cross-reference login times with payroll transaction times. Flag anything that falls outside regular business hours. And we can look for logins from unexpected locations or from devices not usually associated with the authorized users."

Janet and Ted exchanged glances. "We'll get the IT logs right away," Janet said, already reaching for her phone.

It had taken all morning, but Jake finally had a sketch of Robert's face. He snapped a photo and emailed it to the rest of the team. An email reply from the safety manager at Webber Construction asked him to come to their office to discuss his request.

The woman at the front desk paged the safety manager. A few minutes later, Jake found himself in a cramped office with his knees pressed against the back of a cheap wooden desk. The office was full of filing cabinets. The "visitor chair," as the receptionist generously called it, was wedged between a stack of bins and a bookshelf. There was barely enough space for an average person, much less a muscular man like Jake, to sit.

"Hello, I'm Lester P. Felding. The safety manager."

A small man entered the room carrying a black plastic tray in the tips of his fingers. He plopped the steaming tray on his desk, wiped his hands on his pants, and shook Jake's hand.

"How can I help you, Mr....?" The man began making his way around the desk. His slight frame seemed almost tailor-made for the cramped office.

"Mercer. Jake Mercer."

"Oh, yes, you say you are a detective."

"That's correct. Here's my identification."

Lester sat down and peeled a thin layer of plastic off the top of the black tray. The smell of slightly burnt turkey, gravy, potatoes, and stuffing filled the room. Lester held his reading glasses up to his eyes without putting them on to look at Jake's credentials.

"Thank you, Mr. Mercer. I can't be giving out information to just anyone who asks for it."

"Of course not," said Jake, wondering how many people asked for the names of construction workers on a regular basis.

"Now, what do you allege that one of our employsh haf dun?" Lester stuffed potatoes in his mouth before he finished speaking.

"Oh, no, sir, you misunderstand. I'm looking for a worker who may be able to provide an alibi for a female delivery driver whom we believe has been wrongly accused of theft. The man I'm looking for would be a smoker who was working on a construction site on the evening of January 8th."

Lester continued eating as he spoke. "Lemme see. I can look up the date here and see all the projects we have...Where was the construction site?"

"I believe it was on the east side of town. That's all I know."

Lester slapped a hand on the table and started nodding as

he chomped on turkey. He grabbed a pen and started scribbling on a sheet of paper. He wiped his mouth on his sleeve before handing the paper to Jake.

"Lucky for you, only one project was running in town that night. Over on 10th street near the park. These are the names of the twelve men who were onsite that night."

"Only twelve?"

"Yeah, it's a small project and we don't want too many men out at night in this weather."

"You put a star next to the name Ben Williams?"

"That's right," Lester said through a mouthful of stuffing. "He's the project super."

"Do you know how I can get in touch with him?"

Lester shook his head and waved toward the door as he grabbed his ringing phone and started talking through another mouthful of stuffing. Jake gratefully unfolded his long legs and left the room. Twelve possibles wasn't too bad. Now he needed to narrow it down to one. He stretched his arms over his head and cracked his back.

"Excuse me, ma'am?" Jake addressed the woman at the front desk. "Would you be able to help me find contact information for Ben Williams?"

"Hon, I can do you one better." The woman picked up her phone and punched a few buttons.

"Ben Williams to the front desk. Ben Williams. Please report to the front desk." Her voice echoed around the cavernous space as it came through the intercom. A husky man in jeans and a long sleeve plaid shirt approached the desk.

"Mr. Williams? I'm a private detective."

The man turned on his heel and bolted. Jake was surprised, but his training kicked into high gear. He lunged forward and reached out. His fingers grazed the man's shoulder as momentum carried him out of reach. Williams dashed to the far end of the empty lobby. He tried desperately to push open the heavy glass exit door. Jake's long legs let him overtake the runner with ease. He grabbed the man's shoulders and swung him up against the wall, away from the door.

Panting heavily, Ben Williams put up his hands and started begging. "I've sent the next payment, I promise, it won't happen again, please…"

Jake loosened his grip but placed his hand on the man's chest. "Calm down, I just want to talk. I don't know anything about the payments."

"You…My wife didn't send you?"

"No, Mr. Williams. I'm here to ask about the men on your crew working January 8th. I'm looking for a potential eyewitness to help my client." Jake noted the relief on the man's face and hoped this deadbeat dad was not his witness.

But, of course, he was.

Fortunately, Mr. Williams clearly remembered taking a smoke break with a lovely young woman who was also a delivery truck driver. He even managed to get her phone number, so that corroborating piece of evidence should help his testimony hold up. Mr. Williams typed out and signed a witness statement. He gave the detective his contact information and agreed to testify if needed.

Jake smiled as he thought about handing the witness statement over to Maggie when he got back to Baltimore. With any luck, it would be the final piece in the puzzle for proving her client innocent of the charges.

13

The sun was beginning to peek out from behind the winter clouds as Katherine entered Johns Hopkins' Bio-engineering and Medical Research building. She followed the signs to locate Dr. Kevin Mahoney's office and knocked on the door. A middle-aged man in a long white coat answered and waved her inside.

"Yes, come in. I've heard from my colleagues that you've been asking questions around campus. I knew it would only be a matter of time before you came to me. Please, have a seat."

Dr. Mahoney's office looked less like a university professsor's office and more like a medical doctor's patient room. The antiseptic smell added to the illusion. The man himself was average height and weight, but his piercing blue eyes crackled with energy and insight.

Katherine sat in the uncomfortable plastic chair the professor indicated, while he sat on a round rolling stool behind a long metal table which seemed to serve as his desk.

"Thank you, Dr. Mahoney. Obviously, you've heard about our investigation."

"Yes, Dean Yoseff called me last night and filled me in on the details. How can I help?" Dr. Mahoney rolled his stool around from behind the desk and Katherine fought the urge to say 'ah.'

"As Olivia's thesis advisor, I suspect you know her best. How would you describe her?"

"Intelligent. Passionate about her research work. Single-minded in focus. At least she was before Robert entered the picture."

"I've heard that her grades were slipping. Do you think her relationship was distracting her?"

"Yes and no. Her grades were dipping slightly, but she's still my highest scoring student. If anything, her relationship with Robert has increased her passion and dedication, which translates to increased production in the lab."

Katherine was surprised. This information did not align with what other teachers had told her, but Dr. Mahoney was the one closest to Olivia. "That's interesting. Most people I've spoken with have seen Robert as a distraction or worse."

"Sometimes scientists and academics have a tendency to get locked into our ivory towers at the expense of a social life."

"So you didn't see any issues in the relationship?"

"On the contrary, I think their relationship was good for Olivia. It took her out of her studies some, yes. But it's healthy for a young woman to pursue social activities. It's something we discussed often. Olivia has the potential not only to be a great scientist but also to help bridge the gap between science and the people we are working to help. I encouraged her to make more friends, reconnect with family, and even to 'get out there' on the dating scene. I was pleased that she found Robert and never anything but impressed by the way her treated her."

Katherine regarded the professor thoughtfully. She admired his quiet strength. "I appreciate your perspective, Dr. Mahoney. I hope your students appreciate having you as a mentor."

The doctor's face flushed slightly and he cleared his throat.

"What can you tell me about Robert?"

"Robert is very protective of Olivia. And above all, I am quite sure that he is an honorable man."

"Are you aware that he lied about being registered for classes here at the university?"

"Dean Yoseff told me she wasn't able to locate Robert's student record. I don't know what to tell you about that, but I don't believe Robert is a con artist. They have disagreements like any couple, but Robert truly cares about Olivia. There must be a logical explanation for the missing records."

Katherine sat back in her chair. If this discerning professor had faith in Robert, maybe they should reconsider whether he was involved. He had some questions to answer, but he wasn't their only suspect.

"You mentioned that they have disagreements? Do you know anything about the argument they had on Friday?"

"You've heard the rumors." The professor pressed his lips together and rubbed his chin.

"Do you know what the fight was about?"

Dr. Mahoney nodded. "I was in the cafeteria when it happened. I couldn't hear everything, but the conflict was about her father disapproving of their engagement."

"Since you were there, can you describe the actual events? I've heard a mix of theories and rumors." Katherine pulled a small booklet out of her pocket to take notes.

The professor took a deep breath. "Let me set the record straight. Last Friday, Robert and Olivia sat at their usual table in the corner of the cafeteria away from everyone else. Suddenly, their voices started getting loud. Olivia got up and walked out of the place. It surprised me because she doesn't show anger like that. Robert was following her saying, 'Olivia, wait!' I looked out the window as they went outside and Robert caught her."

"Caught her?"

"Yes, he reached out and grabbed her arm. From their body language, it seemed clear to me that they were both very upset. I went outside to find out what was wrong and suggest that they give each other some space. By the time I got there, Olivia had already walked away. Robert was staring off in the direction I assume she went. He was frowning and his shoulders slumped. I don't think he even noticed me standing there."

"What did he do then?"

"He just turned toward the parking lot and left."

"Did you see him get into his car? What kind of car does he drive?" Katherine asked.

"I did see him get into a car, but I can't tell you much about it. I'm not a car guy. It was big, an SUV I guess, and blue. Almost navy blue. Other than that, I can't really say." The professor lifted his shoulders.

"Was that the last time you saw Olivia?"

"Yes, it was. I had hoped to see her later Friday afternoon, but she didn't show up."

Katherine's ears perked up. "She missed an appointment with you?"

"No, not exactly. Every few weeks I have a gathering for my grad students, just to chat and socialize with each other. I usually order pizza and we hang out in the student lounge. But students aren't required to come. I wasn't too surprised she didn't come, though I did want to speak with her. As upset as she was after the argument with Robert, I figured she needed some space to think for herself and decide what she really wanted."

"Do you have any idea at all where she could be now? I will respect her privacy when I find her, but her father is desperately worried. I need to reassure him that she is safe."

"I appreciate your dilemma, detective. If I knew where she might have gone, I would tell you. I believe she would want to go away to get some fresh air and a fresh perspective. Beyond that, I don't know where she might be."

"You don't seem concerned about Olivia's whereabouts."

"No. As a matter of fact, I would be surprised if you didn't find her this afternoon, in the lab on the other end of this building. That's where the students have an open lab meeting on Tuesdays. Olivia never misses it. I'm sure she'll turn up."

"I hope you're right, Doctor. Please call me if you hear from Olivia or remember anything else that could be important." Katherine handed the professor her business card as she left.

Walking through the building, she wondered where Robert might have gone in his dark blue SUV. Did he give Olivia her space? Did he try to follow Olivia to reason with her? Did he show up at her apartment Friday evening to—

"Oh!"

Katherine stopped short as a young woman ran into her with a soft thud.

"I'm so sorry!" The woman exclaimed, her eyes widening in embarrassment. She stumbled back a step.

"No harm done," Katherine assured her. "Are you okay?" Katherine recognized the beautiful light brown skin and dark curly hair from one of the photographs she had seen when they searched Olivia's room.

Donna had a stack of papers precariously balanced in her arms. "Yeah, just a little clumsy sometimes." She started to stoop down to retrieve the pen she'd dropped.

"Please, let me." Katherine picked it up.

"Oh, thank you! I'm Donna, by the way. Donna Applegate."

"Hi, Donna! I'm glad I ran into you." Katherine chuckled. "I'm Katherine Carson. I have some questions about a friend of yours. I was on my way to the open lab group."

"Oh, well, you've nearly found us! Follow me. We can talk once I get these papers put down."

14

Katherine followed Donna the rest of the way to the lab, smiling at her exuberance. Donna talked faster than she walked, rattling on about the building and the rooms they passed. She explained the open lab was for both undergrad and graduate students in bio-engineering and related fields. They would use it to exchange information and run simulations of their theories.

As they approached the lab door, Katherine saw four young people in white lab coats through the window. Two were working at computer consoles, and the other two were standing near a microscope. Donna went to a table to put down the disarrayed stack of papers she was carrying. Katherine caught part of the conversation happening around the microscope.

"... viable organs. The tissue needs to be stabilized."

"I disagree. My technique will save significant time and cost. Further precautions will only slow the process without providing a significant increase in benefit."

Katherine approached the two men as they continued their discussion. She recognized the taller student as Gordon, whom she'd met in Dean Mary Yoseff's office yesterday. They looked up when she cleared her throat.

"Yes?" Gordon, the one who wanted to save time and cost, seemed annoyed by her interruption.

Donna bobbed over to them, her tightly coiled ebony curls bouncing along with her. "This is Gordon and Ivan. Katherine was coming to here to talk to us about…" Donna giggled. "Oops! I just realized I'm not even sure what you want to talk about!"

Katherine pulled a photo of Olivia from her pocket. "Do you recognize this woman?"

Donna snatched the photo for a closer look. "Oh my gosh! It's Olivia! You must be the private detective."

"That's right. It seems no one has seen her since she and her boyfriend made a scene here on Friday."

"I hope nothing has happened to her," Donna said. "The program wouldn't be the same without her!"

"That's for sure." The other young man spoke up. "I'm Ivan Rosen." He loosely shook Katherine's hand.

"Good to meet you, Ivan. I take it you know Olivia, too."

"Yeah, I've worked with her quite a bit here in the lab, even though we're in different programs."

"That's why you like her." Gordon wrinkled his eye-brows as he grew more annoyed. "If you were in bio-engineering instead of bio-med, she wouldn't be so easy to get along with."

"Don't listen to Gordon." Donna leaned in close to whisper to Katherine. "He's jealous because Olivia's got him beat. He's been in the program for four years already and hasn't been able to finish his thesis. Olivia's is almost finished and she's only been here two years."

Katherine was impressed. "Is that what you are working on here? Bio-printing?"

"That's right! We mainly focus on developing the technology

from an engineering perspective. But we have big dreams for how it will be used in the future." Donna led Katherine around the lab and explained more about their research. The guys stayed huddled at their microscopes.

"The end goal is to be able to create biologically viable human organs that can be used in organ transplants," Donna explained.

"That sounds ambitious."

"Oh, it is. We are likely years away. But, once the technology works, we hope to print organs on demand. They will match a patient's unique genetic and physical needs. This will cut transplant wait times and the risk of organ rejection. Olivia is especially passionate about this subject. You know her mother died waiting for a kidney transplant."

"I heard. I imagine that drives Olivia to work so hard."

"It does. I got into this field because I found it interesting, but Olivia is a true believer—an idealist!" Donna smiled as she led the detective back around to the microscope area.

"And how about you, Mr. Jones? Why did you choose this program of study?" Katherine thought she saw Gordon's face flush slightly.

"That's my business." Gordon shifted his weight. "I chose this program for lots of reasons."

"He means lots of money." Ivan elbowed him in the ribs and laughed. "Me, too. Medical research is a lucrative business ... and if we can save a couple lives along the way, so much the better."

"Of course, the most lucrative positions go to innovators," Gordon said. "Those of us who make discoveries first."

Donna rolled her eyes and flounced her curls. "Leave it to them to make lifesaving technology a profit-driven enterprise."

Katherine shook her head and laughed softly. "It takes all kinds. I do appreciate the tour, but I really came to find out more about Olivia. Are you very close?"

"Oh, of course! Olivia is a gem," Donna gushed. "We've been friends since I moved here for school. We graduated together, and now we get to work together on our graduate studies."

"That's great. When did you all last see her?" Katherine looked around at the group.

Donna answered first. "Friday at the library. I was studying and she was volunteering. We just waved hello since it was busy then." Her eyes clouded. "I hope that isn't the last I see of her."

Ivan patted Donna on the shoulder. "Don't worry, Donna, the detective here is going to find her, right?"

"Yes, I am."

"See?" Ivan looked back to Katherine. "I haven't seen Olivia since last Tuesday's lab, but that's not unusual since we don't have any classes together."

Katherine smiled her thanks and turned to Gordon who was glaring into a notebook. She cleared her throat.

Gordon growled. "I haven't seen her since Tuesday either."

Katherine's eyebrows climbed. "You don't have any classes together?"

Gordon tilted his head toward her and spoke condescendingly. "None of our classes started this week. We have a weekly meet-up with Dr. Mahoney on Friday, but I was busy. So, I don't know whether she showed up or not."

"Thank you, Mr. Jones." Katherine turned back to Donna. "What can you tell me about Robert?"

"Oh, Robert's a doll! He always treats Olivia like a lady."

"No problems, suspicious behavior?"

"None that I noticed." Donna shrugged.

"So, as far as the three of you know, Olivia and Robert have a good relationship. Would they have anything to fight about?"

"You mean the fight in the cafeteria. Every couple fights," Donna said. "Her dad didn't approve of their relationship. She was conflicted. She's so close with her dad, but she wanted a future with Robert. We've talked about going away on a girl's trip over spring break so she could think things through."

"Where did you talk about going? Could Olivia have gone there on her own if she needed space?"

"Are you kidding?" Ivan said. "I can't imagine Olivia going away even for a weekend, much less a week. Donna would have to drag her kicking and screaming." He snickered.

"Oh, come on, she's not that bad. She's just dedicated," Donna said. "And she's the brightest lightbulb in this box, let me tell you! She's the hardest worker you'll ever meet. She is going to make big things happen someday!"

"We all will." Gordon cut her short. "Don't listen to the fangirl. Olivia's a good student, sure, but she isn't any smarter than the rest of us."

"Tell me more."

"Well, I don't know what to tell you. She always has her nose in a book. She never goes to parties, not even with us. A real loner. Doesn't like to share her research."

"That's not true," said Ivan. "She doesn't usually share her raw notes, but she'll share her sources and discuss her conclusions any time. How about that paper from last year?"

Gordon rolled his eyes. "She's so obsessed with helping people. I still don't understand why it matters whether farm workers can be viable organ donors."

Ivan laughed. "If people are scared to get organ donations

from other people, then that makes our research even more important. Get her paper in the right people's hands and I bet we could drum up a new government research grant."

Katherine tried to get the conversation back on track. "Do any of you know where Olivia might be if she isn't here?"

Donna said, "I've heard the rumor that she stormed off to get away from her boyfriend. But she loves this open lab time. It's very unusual for her not to show up. I don't know where she would go."

"I can't help you," Gordon said. "Outside this lab, I didn't have much to do with her. She was spoiled and stuck up. Now you'll have to excuse me. I have important work to attend to." Gordon turned back to his microscope.

"Don't listen to him. Olivia and Gordon used to be close. He used to have a crush on her, until he realized she was going to outshine him with her research." Donna raised the pitch of her voice. "It seems to me that there is enough room in the field of bio-printing for more than one researcher ..."

Ivan smirked, "There will be soon enough."

"Thank you, Donna, you've been very helpful. Ivan, thank you. Mr. Jones," Katherine tapped the young man on the shoulder to give him her card. "If you think of anything that might be of help, please call me."

"Why don't you go bother someone else? Like the guy parked outside her window the other night? I don't know anything about where she might be or who she might be with."

"You saw someone at Olivia's apartment that night?"

"I ... No. I've never been to Olivia's apartment. I thought you said her boyfriend picked her up. I don't know anything, I'm just trying to make the most of the time before she gets back. Assuming she does come back." Gordon spun away and stormed out the lab door.

15

When Katherine exited the building, Lee waved from the other side of the quad. He jogged in her direction. "Katherine! Wait up!"

"Hey, did you find anything?"

"A few more shots of your friend Marty, not much else. No sign of Olivia after Friday afternoon. Of course, the cameras here only cover the main entrances, academic records, and financial offices. It was dumb luck I spotted Marty the first time."

Katherine chuckled. "Speaking of Marty, I need to remind him about getting me copies of his reports on Olivia."

"We've also got another potential lead. Jake put me in touch with Ames Enterprises' CFO and the agent in charge of the investigation into the salary fraud. These schemes often leave traces, no matter how careful the perpetrator is."

"What did you find?" Katherine could see the excitement in her friend's eyes.

Lee motioned with his gloved hands to illustrate his words. "I spotted a series of transactions that were timed to process when the system was least monitored. Then, I compared the login data with the suspicious payroll transactions. I found multiple logins from a single Device MAC Address at the exact times of the transactions. And this unique identifier wasn't connected to any known employee device."

Katherine's eyes widened. "Who does it belong to?"

"The FBI traced the IP address to an apartment house in Wilmington leased to a man named Bailey Anderson." Lee put his hands in his pockets. "Hard to say if he's got anything to do with our missing person, but since his payroll scheme was discovered, he could have a grudge against the company."

Katherine tilted her head to the side. "I imagine he's long gone by now, he's had several months' head start."

"True. He apparently cleared out of his apartment hours after the fraud was discovered. But now that they have a name, the FBI will start tracking down his contacts and tracing his assets. It might give us another motive."

"Yoohoo! Hello there!" A third voice intruded on their conversation. Katherine turned to see an athletic older woman with frizzy gray hair approaching. The woman juggled an armload of books and seemed to be having trouble keeping her glasses on her nose.

"Hello, Ms. Nichols." Lee helped the woman with her books as he introduced her. "This is my partner, Katherine."

Ms. Nichols grabbed Katherine's hand in both of hers and shook it energetically. "Oh! It's so nice to meet you! Leroy here was telling me all about you when he came to visit me and Fluffy yesterday!"

"Well, that was too kind of Leroy, wasn't it?" Katherine

smiled in Lee's direction as he struggled to shuffle the books into a more manageable stack.

"Oh, yes! We had such a lovely chat. You really must come back and visit soon, my dear." Ms. Nichols patted Lee's elbow, then tried to smooth down her frizzy curls.

"Thank you, ma'am," Lee said. "Is there something we can do for you?"

"I'd almost forgotten in all the excitement! I saw you out here and just had to come tell you what I discovered today, seeing as you were so interested in dear Olivia."

The laughter rushed from Katherine's face. "Did you remem-ber something?"

"No, I found something. These books!" She pointed at the stack of books in Lee's arms, a look of triumph on her face.

Lee and Katherine looked at each other blankly.

"You don't understand." Ms. Nichols rushed to explain. "These books were in the *library*. Can you believe it? Right there in the book return slot! Must have been dropped off last night. They weren't there yesterday. I couldn't believe my eyes, but I gathered 'em up and set them aside for my handsome detective friend." Ms. Nichols smiled—a little too warmly—at Lee.

Katherine's humor had returned. She struggled to keep her lips closed against the laugh that rumbled in her chest.

Lee replied, "Ah, thank you, Ms. Nichols. I'm afraid I'm not much of a reader."

"Oh." The librarian sounded deeply disappointed, as if her prince charming had just turned into a toad. "Well, these books aren't for you to read anyway. They are evidence." She hissed out the last word.

"How so?" asked Katherine.

"Oh, didn't I explain?" Ms. Nichols put her hands on her hips. "There I go again, putting the cart before the horse."

"That's okay." Katherine put her hand on the woman's shoul-der. "What makes you think these books are evidence?"

"These are the books that Olivia Ames has had checked out of the library for the last two weeks."

"You found them in the book return slot?" Katherine asked.

"Yes! Which is why I've changed my mind."

Katherine prompted, "Changed your mind?"

"Oh, yes. Something is certainly wrong."

"What's wrong?" Katherine looked at Lee, who shrugged a silent "told ya' so."

"Well, Olivia checked these books out two weeks ago, and they were due yesterday. Technically, putting them in the book drop last night means they aren't overdue."

"I see." Katherine didn't see.

"Don't patronize me, young lady, I know what I'm talking about. Olivia would never put books into a book drop. Never. She loves books far too much. The library is open until 11:00 pm on Mondays, which should have given her plenty of time to return the books to the circulation desk. And for that matter, she could have called to renew them for another two weeks if she needed them longer." Ms. Nichols nodded her head vigorously.

Lee risked a question. "Could someone else—"

"That's what I'm saying! Someone else must have returned the books. But why? Because they were nearly past due. If someone saw the stamp inside the book and realized the books were due, they might not want us calling Olivia to try to track down the overdue books."

"That is interesting." Katherine said, meaning it this time. "Has anyone at the library heard from her?"

"No, we haven't. Olivia usually volunteers on Monday evenings. She helps reshelve the extra books from the weekend and watches the circulation desk while the librarian on duty takes a dinner break. She doesn't have a set schedule, but it's very un-usual for her not to let us know if her plans changed."

"Thank you for your insight, Ms. Nichols."

"Oh, you're welcome, dear. I do hope you find Olivia soon. I believed she must have eloped with Robert, but now I'm not so sure. She was so excited about her future with Robert, I would expect to have heard the happy news by now."

As Ms. Nichols hurried back into the library, the detectives walked to Katherine's car. Lee put the stack of books in her back seat. "That was strange," Lee said.

"I'm not sure 'books in the book drop' is the most solid evidence," Katherine agreed. "But it's something to think about. Who returned the books if it wasn't Olivia? Could she have sent her boyfriend to do it?"

Lee shrugged as he answered his phone. "Hey, Jake. Yeah?"

Katherine checked her phone and saw a text from Sammi. She'd found an address for Susan Campbell and learned that she was employed at Cut Right Salon.

Lee hung up. "Jake found Margaret's witness."

"Oh, that's great news!"

"Yeah, he's going to take the statement to her office." Lee looked at his watch. "I imagine he'll be getting back to town any time now."

Katherine beamed. "Maybe he'll invite Mags out for an early dinner."

Lee laughed. "I wouldn't hold my breath! I've never seen a man move as slow."

"Well, Sammi found the address for one of the people in Olivia's photos. It's not far from here. You wanna come along?"

Lee rubbed his hands together briskly. "Absolutely."

They drove to the address and parked on a street lined with classic Baltimore row-homes. Each one was painted in a unique, bright color.

They walked to the door of number 174 and knocked. Lee stepped over a snow-covered flowerbed to peer into the first-floor window.

"Looks deserted."

"Can I help you?" The question came from a tall, thin man with shaggy blonde hair and pasty white skin. He was standing at the top of the landing of the home next door.

"Hello, sir," Katherine replied, "we're trying to locate Susan Campbell."

"Oh, she and her husband are out of town. I'm watching their place. Anything I can do for you?"

"Perhaps, Mister ..."

"Ames. Victor Ames."

16

"Ames? As in Ames Enterprises?" Katherine asked.

The man snorted. "Only if you consider tending bar an enterprise. I'm one of the poor Ames's."

"Any relation?" Lee stepped back onto the sidewalk.

"None to speak of. Jonathan Ames is my uncle." Victor smirked and rolled his eyes.

Katherine remembered what Sammi said about Victor's unusual activity on Olivia's Facebook page. "Would you be able to spare a few minutes of your time to speak with us? We're private detectives looking into Olivia's whereabouts."

Victor furrowed his eyebrows. "Has Olivia run away? Isn't she a little old for that?"

Katherine stepped down from Susan's landing. "Could we talk about it inside? The wind is piercing."

Victor's brows stayed furrowed. He looked from Katherine to Lee, who was stamping his feet and blowing on his hands. "Alright. Come inside."

As she stepped into Victor's rowhome, Katherine was surprised by the sophisticated looking living room. A sleek entertainment system with a large flat-screen TV dominated one side of the room. She could almost see Lee salivating over the equipment as they removed their coats.

Victor indicated a coat rack behind the door for the detectives to use. A newspaper and coffee cup sat on a glass coffee table, indicating what Victor had been doing before he'd come outside to confront them.

"Have a seat," he said as he sank into the large, inviting sectional.

Katherine noticed the subtle scent of genuine leather as she tried to sit on the edge. The plush couch had other ideas, and pulled her in. She handed a photograph to Victor.

"Olivia? Wow. Haven't seen her since she was a baby. Uncle John kicked us out not long after she was born. She's grown into a pretty thing, hasn't she?" He handed back the photo.

"You should know that. You do follow her on Facebook, don't you?" asked Lee.

"Oh, sure, of course ... I follow all my family on Facebook. My niece taught me."

"It seems like you're pretty interested in Olivia's life. You read everything she posts?"

Victor crossed his arms. "Yeah, so I'm interested. We had a falling out with Uncle John when my mother died. But that didn't have anything to do with Olivia."

"Have you seen or heard anything that might give us a clue about Olivia's whereabouts?" Katherine asked.

"No, I wouldn't know anything about them at all if I didn't see Uncle John's face in magazines occasionally. And Olivia's posts on Facebook, of course."

Lee spoke up. "What was the falling out about? If you don't mind me asking."

Victor sighed. "Yeah, sure. I never knew my uncle well. But

I knew he didn't approve of my mother's lifestyle. She was an actress, always the center of attention. Our grandfather left my mother and my uncle a lot of money. Uncle John took his share and built a successful company. Mom used her inheritance on things that made her happy. All the good things in life."

Katherine noticed an open shelving unit with an impressive assortment of liquor bottles. Many appeared valuable. She took it that Victor had inherited his mother's taste for the finer things.

"We lived with Uncle John and his wife Della for a while after Mom's money ran out. Things were always tense. Then Olivia came along, and he decided it was time for us to move out. We moved a couple times after that and lost touch. Years later, when Mom got sick, things were tough. We didn't have any money, and I didn't know what else to do. I called Uncle to tell him that Mom had died, hoping he might help us out. He told me that Mom had already spent everything she'd inherited, and he didn't owe us anything. That was the last time I spoke to him."

"Your mother was ill?" Katherine had heard about Linda Ames' death, but she wanted to know Victor's perspective.

"Yes. She had liver disease. We thought we were lucky when we found an organ donor for her. But the transplant failed."

Katherine remembered her conversation with Dean Murphy.

"So, what's going on with Olivia?" Victor settled back into the couch and crossed his legs.

Lee said, "We aren't sure yet. She isn't answering her phone and we can't locate her. Her friends are worried."

Victor frowned. "Do you think she's run away? Or was she kidnapped?"

The detectives looked at each other. "We can't discuss an open investigation," Katherine said.

"I can't think of a reason why Olivia would run away from her life. From what I see on Facebook she seems to have it all together. Have the police been called in?"

"At this point, we're just collecting information. Trying to get an idea where Olivia might have gone," Lee said.

"So, you do think she disappeared willingly."

Katherine pursed her lips and changed the subject. "We understand that your neighbor is friendly with Olivia."

"Well, I wouldn't know anything about that. We're neighborly but we don't cross paths outside of the block here."

Katherine asked, "Do you know when she will be back?"

"Susan and Douglas are gone all week. A Southern Caribbean cruise, I understand. Why do you want to talk to her?"

"Well, we want to know if she saw Olivia on Friday before she went missing."

Victor narrowed his eyes. "I know the Campbell's left on Friday. But I can't think of anything else to tell you. This is all very strange. Olivia is an adult. Why are you looking for her if you don't suspect some kind of crime?"

"Again, Mr. Ames, it isn't something we can discuss. Thank you for your time."

"Did you get a weird vibe from that guy?" Lee asked.

Katherine nodded, gripping the steering wheel tightly. "I did. Sammi says he's overly interested in Olivia's Facebook posts."

"He seemed way too well-off for a bartender. And he's bitter toward Jonathan Ames."

"We should dig into his background. Something doesn't add

up." Katherine said. "We better tell Sammi that we found Victor Ames's address so she doesn't need to keep looking for it."

Lee pulled out his phone. "I'll text her now."

As he typed, Katherine continued, "Sammi mentioned that Susan works at the Cut Right Salon. I don't know if that's where they met, but Olivia got her hair done there on Friday. I'm going to take Sammi over to the salon this afternoon to interview the manager."

Lee grinned, putting his phone away. "Nice. It'll be good for her to get some field experience."

"Yeah, I want to do more to train her this year. She has the potential to be a good detective." Katherine smiled, thinking about how eager Sammi was to learn.

"By the way, I just got another update from the FBI on Bailey Anderson. Turns out his apartment is still under contract, prepaid. And they found a file folder of reports and pictures from your old friend, Marty Slye."

"From Marty?"

"Yep. Looks like Bailey Anderson is Marty's mystery client."

Katherine frowned. "Why would a man who engineered a long running financial fraud hire a private detective to follow Olivia? What could he want with that information?"

"The FBI is currently investigating his business holdings. He's got a web of shell companies and offshore accounts to conceal his fraudulent activities. He could be just about any-where in the world right now."

"Except he was in Baltimore just last week. Marty said he paid him in person." Katherine glanced at her passenger.

Lee's eyes went wide. "I need to call Ted right now. That might narrow their search. Maybe Jake can get a description from Marty and—"

"The FBI has their own artists. I need Jake focused on Olivia right now." Katherine's mind raced. "Can your contact get copies of personnel records? We need to find out how Bailey Anderson is connected to Olivia."

Lee raised an eyebrow. "Can't Mr. Ames get them?"

"I haven't been able to get in touch with him, so your line may be faster."

Lee started dialing. "I'll see what I can do. My contact owes me a favor."

Katherine sighed, staring out the window at the bustling city streets. Her gut knew there was something off about the whole case. Why target Olivia? And why go through a private detective like Marty? Maybe Olivia stumbled onto something she wasn't supposed to. Or maybe she's a pawn in a plot against her father. And maybe the incident with Bailey Anderson and Ames Enterprises had nothing at all to do with Olivia's disappearance.

By the time Lee hung up, Katherine found herself hoping that Olivia had eloped with Robert, and that somewhere they were off living happily ever after.

"Ted is going to get a forensic artist in touch with Marty right away. They are also staking out Anderson's apartment, just in case he shows up."

Katherine nodded. "Good. We still have several other avenues to explore. You can do that digging into Victor's background. And we'll see what Sammi and I can find out from the salon this afternoon."

Lee chuckled. "Hopefully Sammi doesn't scare them off with her zealousness."

"She'll be fine." Katherine laughed. "She just needs more practice."

17

The Cut Right Salon was an unimpressive shop located in a strip mall on the west side of the city. As they entered, Katherine was hit by the overwhelming odor of hair and nail care products.

"This isn't the kind of place I would expect an heiress to get her hair done," Sammi whispered.

Katherine had the same thought. But, before she could say so, they were greeted by a curvy middle-aged woman. She wore a tight blue bodysuit under a pink apron with the salon's logo. Her black hair was pulled back in a tight bun, and her light brown complexion was highlighted with plum lipstick and eye shadow.

"Welcome to Cut Right Salon. How can I help you?" She spoke through her nose with a prominent New Jersey accent.

Katherine answered, "Hello, we're here looking for the manager ..."

"That's me, sweetie, manager and owner. Call me Leslie. What can I do for you?"

Katherine pulled several photos of Olivia out of her pocket and showed them to Leslie.

"Do you recognize this woman? We believe she had her hair styled here on Friday."

"You gals ain't cops or something are you?" Leslie took a picture in each hand and looked them over.

"We're private detectives, trying to locate a missing woman." Katherine felt Sammi stand a little straighter beside her.

"Oh, yeah, I remember her. First time she ever came in, far as I know. Got her hair cut by my best girl."

"What is that stylist's name?" Sammi asked the question, then bit her lips together as if she'd spoken out of turn. Katherine winked at her to reassure her she was doing fine.

"Susan Campbell. That's her right here." She pointed a long fingernail at the young woman in the photo they'd taken from Olivia's apartment. "She and your girl here were real friendly. I think they musta already been friends."

"What makes you say that?" Sammi was gaining confidence.

"Well, they weren't just friendly like a client and stylist, ya know? And then something weird happened."

"What?" This time, both detectives asked at the same time.

"Susan finished the job, mighty big transformation as you can see from these photos. I could tell your girl was happy. Then all of a sudden, Susan nipped out of here like she was late to her own funeral. Left your girl there in the chair all covered in hair and all her tools lying ever which where." Leslie gestured wildly with her hands, indicating where Olivia had been sitting and how Susan left.

"I was about to get mad when I noticed your girl..."

"Olivia," Sammi offered.

"Okay, Olivia got up, took off her own apron and started sweeping the hair off the floor. I never saw the like! Then she packs Susan's tools and comes over to talk to me. She said Susan was running late to meet her husband at the airport. Guess they lost track of time. Since your girl—Olivia had kept her late gabbing, she felt responsible and offered to do the cleanup. She paid me and left a generous tip. Then she told me she was going to take Susan's tools home with her and she could pick them up later."

"Was that unusual?"

"Damned unusual. But Susan ran out of here without them, so it's no skin off my nose if they get filched. My girls all provide their own tools and equipment, see? So, if they're careless, they can't blame me."

Katherine nodded. "Do you have any security cameras?"

"Nope. Like I said, 'tain't my fault if someone is careless."

"When is Susan scheduled to be back in the shop?"

"She's not on the schedule until next week." Leslie gave the photos back to Katherine, clearly ready to get back to work.

"Okay, thank you. Does Susan have a cell phone?" Katherine asked.

"She does, but I'm not sure I should give you that ... can I have her call you when she gets back in?"

Katherine could tell arguing was pointless. So, she handed over a business card and thanked Leslie for her help. She and Sammi went back to the car.

"Now what?" Sammi sounded disappointed.

"Well, we need to find out where Olivia went after she left here." Katherine slid into the driver's seat as Sammi got in on the other side.

"It seems like Olivia and Susan knew each other at least since New Year's Eve."

"How do we know that?" Sammi asked.

"Leslie just identified the other woman in the photo as Susan. And Olivia marked the photo as being New Year's Eve 2009."

Sammi brightened up. "I get it! They either met and became fast friends at the party or they already knew each other. I can dig deeper into her social media for a party invite. I still need to go through her Facebook messages, too."

Katherine rubbed her neck. "I know research isn't the most glamorous or exciting part of the job, but I've never meant to sideline you. Just think, you could be helping Lee watch surveillance footage!"

"Yikes! I guess being the office assistant has some benefits after all!" Sammi giggled, then got more serious. "Thank you again for letting me tag along."

"You won't be an assistant forever. You handled yourself well in that interview. Maybe this year I'll have you tag along more often. Then when you have a little more experience, we can see about getting you your own license."

"A P.I. license?" Sammi couldn't hide her excitement.

Katherine chuckled as she pulled up to the curb in front of the Mt. Vernon Business Center. She loved the young woman's enthusiasm. "Yep. But in Maryland, we're 'private detectives.'"

Sammi flashed a grin and jumped out of car. She jogged up the steps of their building.

Before Katherine could get out of the car, her BlackBerry rang with a call from an unknown number.

"Detective Carson? This is Donna Applegate."

Katherine heard distress in her voice. "Donna, is something wrong?"

"Olivia didn't show up for lab today. And her boyfriend Robert just came here looking for her. Where could she be? She never misses lab!"

"You say Robert was there looking for her? When?"

"Just a few minutes ago. He came in asking about her. I told him that no one had seen her since Friday, and there was a detective asking about her and—"

"Did he say where he was going?"

"No, but he hurried out of here. He seems worried too."

"Thanks, Donna."

Katherine ended the call abruptly and called Jake.

"Robert was on campus a few minutes ago."

"On it." Jake shifted lanes and swung his car around to head toward campus. "What happened?"

As Katherine described the phone call, Jake accelerated through several yellow lights and raced to campus. He saw a navy-blue Chevy Trailblazer turning out of campus onto Charles Street. Acting on instinct, Jake floored the accelerator to pass and cut in front of the Trailblazer. Then he slowed down and looked in the rear-view mirror. As he suspected, the man in the driver's seat matched his witness sketch.

"Katie, I've got him. Now it's just a matter of time."

At the next light, Jake made a sharp left turn. He circled the block so he could come up behind the suspect vehicle. The after-noon sun cast long shadows as Jake weaved through narrow streets, his eyes fixed on the blue Chevy Trailblazer ahead. He kept a safe distance at each turn, careful not to draw attention to himself as he tailed Robert through the maze of honking cars and pedestrian crosswalks.

Jake noticed something familiar about the way the Trailblazer navigated the urban landscape. He weaved in and out of traffic, circled buildings, and varied his speed. Once, Jake thought he'd been spotted. Adrenaline surged through him as he dropped further behind.

As they rounded a corner, Jake's heartbeat quickened. The thrill of the chase. He saw Robert pull into a narrow alley lined with towering buildings. Jake drove past the alley and whipped around the side of the adjacent building. He looked back across the street just in time to see the blue Trailblazer come to a stop in front of a dingy office building. Its windows were partially obscured by grime and neglect.

Jake circled the block to find a parking space while he called Katherine back.

"Kat, I followed Robert to the corner of Linwood and Dillon."

"Where did he go?"

Jake parked before he answered, taking a deep breath. He knew what he had to say would send his friend reeling. "He went into the Silo, Katie. Robert works for the Company."

18

The Company.

The words echoed in Katherine's mind. She had severed most of her ties to the CIA and intelligence agencies like it years ago. Now, the thought of them mixed up in her case—her simple, straightforward missing persons case—made her nauseous.

Espionage was a necessary evil, but the secrets and darkness had nearly consumed Katherine in the past. She was haunted by memories of those she had lost. Those that had been taken.

Katherine took a deep breath. If Jake was right...

Of course he's right.

Jake was an accomplished detective and a talented operative. Unlike Katherine, he hadn't cut his ties to the intelligence com-munity. He still consulted with various US intelligence agencies, providing them with insight from his years of experience. At 48 years old, Jake was past his prime for work in the field, according to the NSA. *Their loss.* Katherine was thrilled to have him on her team. And if that meant loaning him out now and again, so be it. But he always kept his consulting separate from their detective agency.

"Katherine. Are you there?" Jake asked. The quiet concern in his voice kept Katherine from spinning further.

She let out a slow breath. "Yeah, I'm here."

"I picked up Robert's trail on campus after you called. And I trailed him to the CIA's training facility downtown."

"Are you sure it's him?" *A silly question. Jake wouldn't make that mistake.*

"Positive. He was using standard, by-the-book evasion tactics to get there. It explains why we've had such a tough time finding out anything." Jake's voice remained measured and calm.

"Yes, I suppose it does. But now I have even more questions."

"Do you want me to reach out to him through my contacts?"

Katherine hesitated. "Not yet. I think we need to talk to him in person before we bring the agency in on this. Stay on his tail. I want to know how all this ties in with our missing lady, but I don't want to tip him in case they're involved."

"Will do."

Katherine hung up the phone. She had joined Sammi and Lee in the office. Lee had just finished telling her that Victor Ames had no criminal history when Jake's call came in. She motioned for Lee to come closer. "We know a little more about the 'boyfriend' now. It seems he's connected to the CIA. Jake thinks he may be an agent."

"Well, that's a wrinkle," Lee said dryly.

"That's an understatement." Katherine crossed her arms and began pacing. Her mind flooded with possibilities. "First of all, if Robert is a CIA agent, why is he operating in the US? The CIA has no authority here."

"No, but agents still live here." Lee reasoned. "And this is a college town. The CIA does recruit agents and analysts while they're in college."

Katherine paused. "Of course. We know Olivia is making huge strides in her research field. I'm sure there's a government application for bio-printing. Maybe Robert was recruiting her. This whole boyfriend persona could have been a cover."

"That's possible," Lee agreed.

"And if she was being recruited, Olivia might have rejected their advances and that could have caused her to run away." *Or triggered them to make her disappear,* Katherine thought.

Lee pressed himself against a file cabinet to get out of Katherine's way as she started pacing again. "If that were true, I think she would have run away before now. She and Robert have been a couple for over a year."

Katherine chewed her lip and snapped her fingers as she thought. "You're right. That's a long time to wait. But she could have been playing hard to get, or maybe she objected to their plans for her research."

"At least we can safely say that CIA involvement explains why she kept her father out of the loop about what was really going on. And why Robert has been so hard to nail down."

"This brings up so many more questions." Katherine counted them off on her fingers. "Did she know or suspect he's an agent? Did the agency know about this relationship? Is the relationship real? Is it real for both of them?"

"The only people who know those answers are Robert and Olivia."

Katherine rubbed her forehead. "Right. Jake is going to follow him. I need to think on the best way to bring him in."

If the CIA was involved with Olivia's disappearance, getting answers was not going to be an easy task. And Katherine knew from bitter experience that pressing them on it might jeopardize more than Olivia's safety.

Sammi cleared her throat. "So, um, do you want me to keep going through Olivia's computer or ...?"

"Yeah, go ahead. If there's anything classified, it would be encrypted." Katherine looked at the clock above the door. "Scratch that. Better wait until tomorrow. Don't want you to be late for family dinner."

Sammi looked at the clock and said, "Oh, thanks. I'd better head out. I did find Facebook messages between Olivia and Susan Campbell talking about New Year's Eve plans. Olivia was keen to meet the rest of Susan's family and Susan said she knew a local bar that had a great party."

"Which bar?" Lee asked.

Sammi shook her head as she put on her coat. "I don't know. They made plans to meet at Susan's apartment and go from there. I've started a list of local bars that do a New Year's Eve event, but it's a long list."

"Good work, Sammi. Back on it tomorrow, yeah?" Katherine smiled at her assistant as the young woman left the office.

Jake parked half a block away and watched for his target to exit the building. He also held a copy of the Sun and turned the page now and then so no one would be suspicious of his presence.

At least, not for a while.

He had waited just under an hour when Robert came outside and got back into his navy Trailblazer. Jake pulled onto the street behind his target and followed at a discreet distance. When Robert parked near an apartment building, Jake continued past. He pulled up at the gas station next door.

Jake texted the address of the apartment building to Lee and Katherine. Then he swiped his credit card and began pumping gas, watching Robert from the corner of his eye. It looked like he was talking on his cellphone. Jake shut off the gas pump when the young man got out of his car and walked toward the apart-ments. Jake left his car where it was and followed.

He saw Robert enter a breezeway, heading for the back of the building. Jake paused at the foot of the exterior staircase and peered through the gaps in the wooden steps in time to see Robert whip around the far corner of the building.

Jake stepped around the staircase, hugging the wall, and crept toward the end of the breezeway. He paused at the corner and listened. Slowly, he turned his head to peek around the corner.

A fist smashed into Jake's gut, knocking him backward. Robert whirled around the corner and thrust his foot into Jake's stomach again, knocking him down to the pavement under the stairs. Caught off guard, Jake pulled his weapon and tried to speak, but the enraged operative kicked the gun out of his hand and grabbed him by his jacket collar.

As the gun skidded across the pavement, the young man slammed Jake against the brick and demanded, "Who the hell are you? And what have you done with Olivia?"

Jake wheezed, "Private detective." He coughed and gasped for air, feeling older than he had in a long time.

Robert reached inside the detective's coat to look for his ID. Jake took the opportunity to grab the younger man and spin him into the wall. Robert raised his fists to start fighting. Jake pulled his ID card out of his back pocket and held it in front of his opponent's face.

"I'm not here to fight you, kid. I'm trying to find your girlfriend."

Jake stood still while Robert snatched the ID and squinted at it for a moment before he released the tension in his shoulders. Then he looked both ways and motioned for Jake to follow him into his apartment.

Jake picked up his gun and put it back into its shoulder holster. He followed Robert into the small studio apartment. Robert sat in a folding chair next to a card table and pointed for Jake to sit.

"Tell me what's going on," Robert demanded.

Jake eased into the other chair and groaned. "You first. I'm not the one who attacked."

Robert furrowed his eye brows. "I have a right to defend my privacy."

"Sure you do, kid. But I'd wager that the Company doesn't appreciate their agents drawing attention to themselves by attacking every private detective, cop, or other rogue who happens to come around."

Robert's face blanched. "You know about the Company? How long have you been following me?"

"Long enough." Jake leaned back in the chair to stretch his sore muscles. "You spotted me when we turned onto Monument Street, didn't you?"

"Why do you say that?"

"You slowed down enough I had to drop back and then

speed up. I thought you'd made me. But then you led me right to your apartment. Why?" Jake texted the apartment number to his friends.

"I didn't make you." Robert rested his elbows on the table. "I had a feeling, but I didn't catch the tail until we got here. I waited behind the stairs out there and looked through to see if anyone was behind me. And tonight, you were."

Jake nodded his head and let out a slow breath. "Now that we're here, let me introduce myself. I'm Jake Mercer. My agency is looking for your friend, Olivia Ames. She apparently went missing on Friday night, not long after you had a fight with her. I'm ex-NSA, which explains why I know what is in the building at Linwood and Dillon."

Robert went to the refrigerator and pulled out two cans of National Bohemian beer. "It doesn't explain why I didn't spot your tail," he muttered.

"I have a couple explanations for that. One, I learned how to hunt people in the Army Rangers. And two, given the intense display of emotion I just witnessed, you're off your game. You really do love her, don't you?"

Robert handed Jake a beer. "Yeah. I do."

"You think that has anything to do with her disappearance?" Jake asked, pressing the cold beer against his bruised hand.

"I don't know." Robert took a swig. "I don't think so." He sat back down. "I hope not. I didn't even know she was missing until today when I talked to Donna at the lab. She's—"

"I know." Jake held up a hand. "She's how I got on your trail in the first place. I've been looking for you ever since we took the case on Monday morning. We have a lot of questions for you. Assuming you didn't have anything to do with Olivia's disappearance, maybe you can help us figure out what is going on." Jake handed Robert a business card.

Robert took a picture of the card with his cell phone. "I didn't have anything to do with it, trust me. I'll be there."

Jake grinned. "I'm not the one you're gonna have to convince to trust you." He had to admit, Robert seemed sincere and willing to help. After the physical altercation ended, of course. Jake planned to keep the fight to himself. *Katie doesn't need any help disliking this guy.*

Robert got up from the table to answer a knock at the door.

19

Katherine noticed nothing special about the young man who answered the door. *The perfect spy blends in with the crowd.* He was dressed in jeans and an un-tucked polo shirt. Average height and weight. Fair skin. Brown hair cut in a simple flat top. Average. Forgettable. Invisible.

Katherine was pulled out of her musings when Lee put his hand on her back. He nudged her forward into the apartment. Jake was already halfway through making introductions.

"We wanted to check on you, Jake," Lee tilted his head in Katherine's direction, "make sure everything was hunky-dory."

Katherine smirked at Lee's attempt at subtlety. She didn't care if Robert knew she was suspicious of him. "Tell me about your relationship with Olivia Ames, how you came to meet her."

Robert took a deep breath. "I'm a student at Johns Hopkins. I met Olivia in an applied engineering course. We hit it off right away, started hanging out, and fell in love."

"In fact, you are not a registered student. And you were asking questions about Olivia before you even met." Katherine's tone was cold.

Robert shifted and glanced at Jake. "Yes, I was interested in meeting her."

"Why?" Katherine's palms were beginning to sweat.

"Look, I didn't have anything to do with her disappearance. I didn't even know she was missing until today."

"How is that possible? I've been told you two were close." Katherine took a sharp breath and willed her heartbeat and voice to stay steady.

"Yes, we were. Are. We just had an argument on Friday. Our first fight. She was pretty upset, so I just thought she was avoiding me."

"What was the fight about?" Lee asked.

Robert shrugged. "Her father doesn't approve of me."

Katherine stared. *The gall of this man. Acting as if he doesn't know exactly what happened.* "You chased Olivia out of the cafeteria when she tried to leave you."

"What?" Jake looked surprised.

"After the 'argument,' Olivia was seen leaving the premises. Your new friend here followed her out of the building and tried to grab her. Olivia stormed off, and he got in his car. I suspect he was going to follow her."

"No!" Robert said. "I mean, yes, I did try to catch up with her, but after she marched off, I just went home."

"What was the fight about, Mr. Norton? If that is your name." Katherine's eyes narrowed and her heart rate increased.

Jake opened his mouth, but Katherine shot him a look to close it and keep it closed.

"I told you, her father doesn't approve of me, and that made her question our relationship."

"Are you sure that's what made her question your relationship?" Katherine felt her skin becoming hot and clammy.

"Yes, of course, what else could it be?"

"Maybe Olivia found out about the CIA. Maybe she found out who you really are. And maybe she resented being lied to, manipulated, and used." Katherine stepped into Robert's personal space.

Robert's eyes went wide and he looked at Jake. "No, I mean, well, maybe but—"

"Maybe Olivia threatened to tell her father what you were trying to do." The veins in Katherine's temples were beginning to pulse.

"I love Olivia!" Robert shouted.

"Olivia found out that you are an agent and was furious with you." Katherine's breathing became shallow, fast. She clenched and unclenched her hands.

"No, I don't think—"

"I've no doubt that you did not think! Now is the time to start thinking! Tell us where Olivia is." Breathing, urgent. Eyes, wide. Heart rate, maximum.

"I. Don't. Know." Robert emphasized each word, locking eyes with his accuser.

Katherine whirled around and charged at the door.

"Katie..." Jake started to stand, but he was too late.

Katherine burst outside and ran from the apartment. She jumped into her car, eyes burning, temples throbbing. She fought back tears and gasped for breath. She peeled out of the parking lot, tires screeching.

She tore through the city. Her ears were ringing and her heart pounded furiously as if the car were running off her adrenaline instead of fuel. Her mind was nearly empty. Her breathing grew erratic. A small flicker in the back of her mind: a warning light telling her it wasn't safe to be on the road. But muscle memory and emotion were driving the car. She could barely think. Her brain wasn't focused on anything but keeping her alive.

Her conscious mind didn't even know where she was going. She parked and shut off the engine. She stared out at the grassy hill, shrouded in darkness and mist like something out of a horror movie. Suddenly, the right side of her brain caught back up with her, having been left behind in her hurry. It snapped back into place and comprehension washed over her. *Druid Ridge Cemetery.* For a moment her breathing stopped. And then she melted into a puddle of tears with her head slumped forward on the steering wheel.

Jake drove through the dark city streets toward Druid Ridge. He knew where Katherine would be. When she'd stormed out a few minutes earlier, he left Lee to explain the incident while he went after her.

Katherine hadn't had a panic attack like that in nearly two years. In the past, Jake might have noticed the signs and been able to prevent it. He was out of practice.

He pulled up next to Katherine's Ford and looked up at the grim scene in front of him. He turned off the ignition and reached for the heavy-duty flashlight he kept in his glove box. He grabbed Katherine's puffy blue coat before climbing out of his car. She had left it behind in Robert's apartment.

He walked around to Katherine's car and placed his hand on the hood. Still warm. He opened her door, leaned in, and removed her keys from the ignition. He closed and locked the door with a heavy sigh. Pocketing her keys, he began trudging up the hill.

The glow of his flashlight led him down a well-worn path through a maze of stone markers. The moon peeked out from behind the clouds, but the stars remained hidden. Jake saw Katherine up ahead, her arms wrapped around herself to keep the cold at bay. A gentle, frigid breeze blew her light brown hair to one side, making her shiver. She stared at the ground and didn't move as he approached. The beam of light fell across the large gray headstone at Katherine's feet.

DANIEL MICHAEL CARSON, BELOVED HUSBAND

AUGUST 29, 1967 – NOVEMBER 23, 2001

Jake wrapped the coat around Katherine's shoulders. She turned into him and began sobbing again. He wrapped the coat around her and rocked her in a soothing rhythm. They stood there in the cold mist and darkness, with only the sounds of Katie's muffled sobs and the damp smell of fresh earth for company.

Jake waited patiently. For her, he could wait forever. He remembered the first time he'd held her in his arms. She had sobbed then, too. And he'd discovered a piece of himself that had been missing. He'd realized in that moment his life's purpose was to love and protect this girl like his own little sister.

Her sobs subsided, and her breathing steadied.

Then he helped her put her arms into her coat sleeves and walked her to his Jeep.

Katherine stared out the window at the winter sky. She watched the shadows of the city flicker past. Her emotions had been raging so fiercely that she hadn't been able to think. Now in the stillness, her mind raced. She felt embarrassed for her behavior, running out like that. She was frustrated with herself for giving in to the panic attack.

And she couldn't believe she'd ended up at Daniel's grave.

Not again. It never helps.

Daniel's death still stung as though it had happened yesterday. Terrorists may have detonated the bomb that ended his life. But they didn't send him on a dangerous mission without any backup. For that, she blamed the CIA.

As they pulled up in front of her apartment, she let Jake walk her to the door. She gave him one last hug before stepping inside. Looking back. she mustered a small smile. He nodded and smiled back. Then he walked away.

Katherine knew that her car would be back in its place outside her apartment by morning. And Jake would never tell anyone about what happened tonight. He'd been protecting her since the day her parents died. She was only nine, and the young soldier who rescued her had become her only family.

20

Katherine got to the office before the sun was up. She had barely slept, and what sleep she got was plagued by nightmares. Robert's denial was hard to swallow. But if he wasn't involved, then what? She hated how much she'd let this case get under her skin. And if her panic attacks were back ...

Katherine shook herself and set to work at her desk. By the time rush hour traffic was crowding past, she was deep into reading the reports Marty had complied for Bailey Anderson. She thought the man was a menace. But he didn't miss much.

His surveillance was thorough. He tracked Olivia all over town. He noted exact times, routes, and buildings she visited on campus. The entry for December 31 was empty except for a note about his being spotted by Robert.

One report included a candid photo of Olivia and Susan together at a café. Clearly, the two young women were friends. They met for breakfast a couple times in the weeks Marty was tailing Olivia.

Katherine pulled out the photo she'd taken when they were searching Olivia's apartment. The image showed Olivia with long brown hair posing in front of a shelf full of sparkling glassware with a younger woman who they had identified at Susan Campbell. The snapshot gave the impression the girls were out on the town. The inscription on the back indicated that Meg, presumably Megan Russell, was present at the party but not included in the picture.

Katherine let out a long sigh and picked up the phone. She dialed the phone number for Megan Russell found in Olivia's car. The number Sammi had called earlier in the week. The phone rang a few times before Megan answered.

"Hello?" The woman's voice was cautious.

"Hi, Megan. This is Katherine Carson. I'm the owner of a local private detective agency, Carson Investigations. I hope this isn't a bad time."

"Oh, uh, no. It's fine," Megan said. "What is this about, Detective? I think your assistant called the other day, but it was all very confusing."

"I apologize for that," Katherine said. "I just have a few questions for you. It's important for our investigation into Olivia Ames' whereabouts."

"Sure, I guess. What do you want to know?"

"My assistant mentioned that you met Olivia only recently. When was that?"

"Actually, it was a couple weeks ago on New Year's Eve. At a party at one of the local bars."

Katherine looked again at the background of the photo. "With Susan Campbell?"

"Susan?" Megan's tone grew sharper, more alert. "Um, yes."

"You were all three at the same party together?" Katherine pressed, noting the hesitation in Megan's response. "We found a photograph of the three of you during our investigation."

"A photograph? Of the three of us?" Megan's voice reflected genuine surprise. "Where did you get that?"

Katherine smiled when her fib hit home. "We found it in Olivia's apartment."

There was a long pause before Megan responded, "Yes, we were at the party."

"Did you know Susan before the party?"

"Yes. Why are you asking about Susan? Is she in some kind of trouble?" Megan sounded defensive.

"We're just trying to gather information at this point. Even small details can be significant," Katherine explained.

"Well, I liked Olivia. We planned to keep in touch. That's why we exchanged phone numbers."

"But no contact since then?"

Megan sighed, "No, nothing. I wish I could help more, but I really don't know anything."

Katherine sensed the end of the conversation. "Just one more question: Where was this party that you attended?"

Megan laughed nervously. "It was a small local bar. I can't think of the name ..."

"In that case, could you tell me how to contact Susan? She might know."

"Oh! Actually, I do remember. "It's Bailey's. Bailey's Bar. I'd almost forgotten."

"Alright, Megan. Thank you for your time. If you think of anything else, please contact me. Here's my number."

"Okay. Sure. Goodbye, Detective."

Katherine pondered the reason for Megan's evasive answers. Every time she mentioned Susan, the woman on the phone got even more guarded. Katherine could hear it in her voice. She was sure Megan was hiding something crucial to the case, but what? They already knew Susan and Olivia were friends and that Susan had styled Olivia's hair on Friday. She looked back at the New Year's Party photograph, convinced there was more to the story.

Katherine sent a message to her friend Detective Alvarez in Missing Persons to see if she could confirm whether Susan Campbell was really on a cruise. Susan seemed to be the last person to have seen Olivia before she went missing, and Megan seemed to want to keep the detectives away from Susan. Katherine was anxious to find out more about her and any other connections to Olivia.

When Jake got to the office, Katherine was staring out the window at the gray, overcast sky. She clutched her phone in one hand and leaned against the tall built-in bookcase.

"I've checked the hospitals, shelters, and morgues." Jake let his voice rumble with frustration. "No sign of her anywhere."

Katherine closed her eyes and rubbed her temples. "And we don't have access to her bank or phone records. So we can't confirm whether she's on the move or if she's just vanished."

Jake sat on the edge of the desk and focused his gaze on Katherine's weary face. "I found out who runs the local Silo," he said quietly.

Katherine turned to meet his gaze.

"Peter Farthern."

Jake smiled when recognition flickered in Katherine's eyes. He knew Peter was on the short list of people in the intelligence community whom Katherine would trust without question. Even though he worked for the CIA now, Katherine would still think of Peter as an ally.

A slow smile spread across Katherine's face. "You think Peter can vouch for Robert."

Jake stepped closer, "He might also have connections that could help us find Olivia."

"Maybe." Katherine looked back out the window.

Jake was sure she was debating with herself over his suggestion. She held a lot of resentment toward the intelligence community. Especially the CIA. Every interaction with the legendary agency seemed to make it worse.

The rift began decades ago when a jaded liaison officer sold out Katherine and her husband for a large fee. Jake was the one they'd called to help them out of that jam. In fact, they always called him whether they needed a safe place to lay low or a quick extraction from danger.

He was also the one Katherine called the night Daniel was killed. He'd been the one to make the funeral arrangements. He was the one who helped her stay in touch with reality and took her to grief counseling.

And in 2002, when she resolved to give up on espionage and make a fresh start, he was the first one she called then, too. Lee, wrestling with his own demons, had suggested the three of them could start a detective agency. It seemed to be exactly what Katherine needed—a way to use her skills to help people without answering to a system she saw as broken and corrupt.

Before he could press her further, the door opened and Sammi walked in. She glanced around, seeming to sense the heavy atmosphere.

"Morning, everyone," Sammi said, trying to sound upbeat. She hung up her coat and patted the stack of books on the counter by the door. "Where did these come from?"

Katherine answered, "Ms. Nichols gave them to us. They're the books Olivia had checked out, but they were returned on Monday. Possibly by someone other than Olivia."

"That's weird." Sammi dropped her backpack by her desk. She looked back and forth between Jake and Katherine. "Anything else new?"

Katherine nodded her head. "Actually, Marty Slye finally came through. His reports include details about Olivia's daily movements over a two-week period. He even snapped a few photos of Olivia with other people in her life."

"Anything catch your eye?" Jake asked.

"Most of the entries are what we would expect from our investigation. Except one. There's a description of an argument with a classmate that took place in the library a few days before she disappeared. No photos, but I'm sure I know who the classmate is."

Jake raised his eyebrows. "No one told us about that before."

"No. According to Marty's notes, Olivia was alone at the desk on Monday evening while the librarian was having dinner. Then a classmate with 'flaming red hair' came along. They talked for several minutes and their conversation got heated. Looks like Marty was mostly going by body language because they kept their voices too low for him to hear much. But I'm going to need to have another chat with Gordon Jones."

"Sounds interesting," Jake said.

Lee walked in the door and headed for the coffee maker as Katherine continued. "I spoke to Megan Russell again. Sammi, I need you to investigate Bailey's Bar. Specifically, their New Year's Eve Party. Olivia might have been there that night."

"Did you say Bailey's Bar? Now there's a coincidence," Lee said, wrapping his hands around a steaming cup. "The FBI has uncovered some of Bailey Anderson's holdings, including a chain of neighborhood style bars named after himself."

"Bailey's Bar?" Katherine asked.

Lee nodded as he sipped his coffee.

Sammi jotted the name on a sticky note. "I'll see what I can find out about the party. I went through Olivia's emails. Nothing suspicious there. I've also been going through the personnel records Lee sent me. I'm tagging anyone who's had disciplinary action or negative performance reviews."

"Any connections to Olivia?" Katherine asked.

Lee spoke up. "I'm going to dive into that this afternoon. Maybe we can find a connection between Anderson and the Ames' family…"

While the others talked, Jake went to refill his coffee. He pulled down an extra cup and filled it with hot water to make some hot chocolate. He applauded Katherine's resilience. But sometimes she tried to move forward at the expense of dealing with her past traumas.

Jake had kept in touch with all his old buddies in the intelligence community and even consulted on occasion. But not Katie. She hadn't contacted anyone from her past since they'd launched Carson Investigations. And she refused to reply to anyone who reached out to her.

She wanted to stay as far away as possible from the world of espionage, so he protected her. Any time a case required contact with a federal agency, Jake took the lead and let Katherine focus on interviewing the civilian witnesses. Keeping her safe and happy had been his primary goals in life for the last thirty years. He supported her career when she was with ESA, and he'd sheltered her old life when she left it behind.

But what happens when her new world collides with the old one? Maybe he'd been sheltering her too much for too long. One way or another, Katherine was going to have to face up to history with the CIA before this case was over. *If only she'd reach out to Peter.*

21

Katherine was enjoying a mug of hot chocolate when Robert came in. For a moment, her heart clenched, but she pushed the feeling aside.

"So, Robert. We've got to understand your side of the story. Olivia's been missing for almost a week. We know you're CIA, and we don't have time for false narratives."

Robert rubbed his neck. "I've been thinking about this all night, and you're right. There's no time to waste." He took a seat on the nearest couch. "My assignment was to recruit Olivia as an asset because of her bio-medical engineering skills. The agency thought I could get close to her. And I did. Too close. Last week, I asked her to marry me."

Katherine squinted. "Did that cause problems at the agency?"

"No. My supervisor knew and didn't disapprove. Olivia was already willing to work with us before the romance developed."

"But she got angry when you popped the question?" Lee asked, pulling his favorite chair up to the group.

"She was excited. But her father didn't take the news of our engagement well. On Friday, she wanted me to tell him who I really am. We fought because I refused." Robert's face flushed.

"You went after her to try to change her mind," Jake said, making eye contact with Katherine.

Katherine held Jake's gaze for a few seconds before looking away. She wasn't ready to give Robert a pass. "Did you try to contact her over the weekend?"

"Yes, but when she didn't respond, I thought she needed more time to cool off."

Katherine leaned forward. "And now, knowing she hasn't reached out to her father since Friday night?"

"That worries me. She's so close with her dad. As far as I knew, she was going to his house over the weekend as usual."

Katherine took a deep breath and let it out slowly. "Okay, we'll assume you weren't involved in Olivia's disappearance. Could it be related to your assignment?"

"My only assignment right now is recruiting Olivia. I can't imagine that it could be related. Other countries are working on bio-medical applications, but they wouldn't know about me, and Olivia wouldn't defect.

"Enemies out for revenge?" Lee prompted.

"None that could come after Olivia."

"You haven't noticed anyone following you?" asked Jake.

"A local guy was trying to get pictures. He claimed to be a reporter, but I think he was with a gossip magazine. I chased him off." Robert smirked.

"He was actually a local private detective hired to follow

Olivia and report on her movements," Katherine said, perhaps a little too eager to point out his mistake.

"Damn." Robert put his head in his hands. "I'm not even the one who noticed him. My surveillance guy did."

Katherine lifted an eyebrow. "Surveillance?"

"Yeah, for security purposes."

Katherine looked up at Jake. "I'll talk to Peter."

Robert's mouth opened slightly, but he didn't ask the question she could see written on his face. In the cool light of day, Katherine didn't detect any deception in Robert's story. She was skeptical of CIA involvement, but a meeting with the local Director of Recruitment might ease her mind.

Katherine sat in her car, watching the Patapsco River roll by. The parking lot was mostly empty since nearby restaurants didn't open until lunch. She spotted a tall man with rich brown skin rounding the corner. As he came closer, Katherine smiled and stepped outside.

"Sorry I'm late," he rumbled as he pulled her into a bear hug.

"It's good to see you, Peter." Katherine got back into her car and cranked up the heat.

Peter slid into the passenger seat. "I'm glad to hear you're running your own team now, Kat."

"A team of detectives, not spies."

Peter smirked. "Jake Mercer, Lee Stewart, and Katherine Carson ... just detectives?" He laughed. "Well, whatever you call yourselves, helping people is helping people. And it's what you were made to do."

Katherine blushed. "So, what can you tell me about Robert?"

"He's one of the best operatives I've ever trained. He's quick and sharp, but more than that, he's compassionate and empathetic when it counts."

"He says he's in love with Olivia Ames."

"I've heard."

"And?" Katherine pursed her lips and stared at the empty fingers on her left hand.

"These days, the agency doesn't exert as much control over its operatives' personal lives." Peter spoke softly. "I can't change the past, Kat. But you know me. And I'm telling you straight—we didn't have anything to do with Olivia Ames' disappearance. I didn't even realize she was missing until yesterday."

Katherine had every reason to trust Peter. They'd worked together at the Espionage Services Agency for years before he transferred to the CIA. "Can you say the same for Robert?"

"I'm absolutely sure. He's a straight arrow. And he's worried about her. He's probably at the office now combing through our surveillance footage."

"Any chance the surveillance team caught Olivia leaving her apartment on Friday?"

Peter shook his head. "When she had the fight with Robert, she said she wanted to be left alone for a while. So we backed off like she asked."

Katherine gave him a look.

He put up his hands and said, "How would I know she'd disappear after twelve months of calm surveillance?"

Katherine slammed her head back into headrest. "Can we get copies of the footage for the last couple weeks anyway? Maybe there's something we can use."

"I'll expedite the process." Peter reached across the seat and took Katherine's hand. "So, are you back?"

"No. Not yet." She had spent most of her life playing the espionage game. For a long time, she'd wanted nothing but to forget the things she had seen. She wanted to go about her life in blissful ignorance, like millions of people all over the world could do.

Peter climbed out of the car, then stuck his head back in. "If you ever change your mind, we can always use a consultant with your expertise." He winked, shut the door, and stepped back into the shadows.

Katherine leaned forward on the steering wheel. She had to rule out the idea that the CIA was behind the disappearance. And they'd ruled out the premise that Olivia had run away with her boyfriend. What was left? The other possibilities were even more dire.

Katherine pushed through the heavy glass doors of Baltimore police headquarters. The familiar aroma of stale coffee mingled with dust, paperwork and glazed donuts brought back memories of countless investigations over the years.

She approached the front desk where a weary-looking officer sat, typing away at a computer. "I'm here to speak with Detec-tive Alvarez," Katherine said.

The officer glanced up, eyeing her with a mix of curiosity and suspicion. "Do you have an appointment?"

Katherine showed the officer her private detective's license. "Tell her Katherine Carson is here. She's expecting me."

With a reluctant nod, the unfamiliar officer picked up the phone and dialed a number, relaying the message to Detective Alvarez. After a brief exchange, he hung up and motioned for Katherine to follow him.

They wound their way through the maze of corridors, passing by offices filled with detectives poring over case files and evidence.

Detective Camilla Alvarez looked up as Katherine entered her office and smiled. "Kat, I heard from Mary Yoseff. Seems there might be something suspicious about Olivia Ames' disappearance after all."

Katherine took a seat in a wooden chair next to the door and put her hands behind her neck. "About that. The information Ms. Yoseff gave you on Robert Norton…"

"Yes?"

"It's a wash."

"How so?"

"Take it from me, Cam, you'll just be wasting the department's time looking into Norton." Katherine leaned down with her arms on her knees.

Detective Alvarez was familiar enough with Carson Investigations to read between the lines about the reason. "Then you know what happened to the Ames' girl?"

"Evidence in Olivia's apartment seems to indicate she packed her own suitcase and left of her of volition. But I can't shake the feeling that something isn't right."

"What do the people in her life think?"

"Her father is very worried since he can't get in touch with her. The teachers and classmates I spoke to earlier this week weren't worried, until she started missing classes and research appointments. Now, they are getting concerned. Asking questions I can't answer. And her boyfriend…"

"Robert?"

"Yes. He's as confused and worried as everyone else."

Katherine rubbed her temples. "Olivia may have left on her own as the evidence suggests, but it feels more and more likely that something happened to her."

"Well, I was able to get a court order to examine her bank records based on the previously suspicious boyfriend, and since she's been gone five days…"

"And since she's Jonathan Ames' daughter?" Katherine suppressed a grin.

"That didn't hurt." Detective Alvarez handed Katherine a computer printout. "No activity on her account since Friday afternoon. A debit card transaction at Cut Right Salon."

"We've been there. Olivia was friendly with one of the stylists, Susan Campbell. She may have been the last person to see Olivia before she disappeared. She and her husband are supposed to be on a cruise."

Detective Alvarez made a note. "Yes, I did confirm with the cruise line, the Campbells did board the ship."

"No recent large cash withdrawals, I see." Katherine asked as she skimmed the bank records.

"No. And it seems like she makes purchases with her debit card almost every day."

"And then nothing for the last five days?" Katherine handed the printout back to the detective. "Something doesn't track. I don't suppose you pulled her phone records?"

Detective Alvarez flashed a grin and handed her another print out. "Same story as the bank account. Usually very active, and then nothing since she called her dad on Friday night."

"Hmm. What do you think, Cam? You have more experience than I do with missing persons."

"People do run away from their lives. They also get kidnapped. But there isn't any evidence of foul play. You've talked with her father. He'd be the one to get a ransom demand if that was the motive. Does he have any other ideas?"

Katherine shrugged. "Robert was his only idea, and that was a wild goose chase. I haven't heard from him in a couple days."

"Do you have any other suspects?"

Katherine hesitated to name any of their leads suspects. "I learned that a classmate fought with Olivia recently. I'm going to interview him again. He seems hostile toward Olivia, but I'm not sure if he's capable of harming her. There's also a man named Bailey Anderson who may have masterminded the fraud at Ames Enterprises."

Detective Alvarez lifted a perfectly arched eyebrow. "Does he have a connection to Olivia?"

"The FBI is investigating Anderson, but it appears that he hired a local private detective, Marty Slye, to follow Olivia for a few weeks."

"Marty, of all people?" Detective Alvarez rolled hers eyes with a chuckle. "Well, I've filed the missing persons report and put out a full description. Of course, if we find her and she did leave of her own free will, I won't be able to notify her father without her consent. She is an adult."

"Yeah, I know. We just need to know she's safe. And alive."

22

Neither Lee nor Jake had been inside Bailey's Bar before, but nothing about it surprised them. A long mahogany bar on one side of the room sat empty. On the other side, small tables and faded leather booths held a handful of lunchtime guests. The lighting was dim, even though the windows were open. The air was filled with the scent of fried food and beer, and a classic rock station played in the background.

"So, the man who organized a million dollar salary padding scheme also owns a local dive bar?" Jake smirked.

Lee chuckled at his friend's sarcastic tone. "He owns several, up and down the coast. It's a good cover for laundering his ill-gotten gains."

"If Susan is the one who invited Olivia to the party here," Jake said, "then it really could be a strange coincidence that Bailey Anderson was also having Marty follow her."

Lee asked the bartender if they could speak with the manager before he responded. "Or maybe Susan is involved with Bailey Anderson in some way."

They watched the bartender come out of the back room with a shaggy haired man whom Lee recognized immediately. He nudged Jake. "That's Victor Ames! Katherine and I spoke to him yesterday. What's he doing here?"

Victor glanced up. His eyes widened momentarily before he smiled and walked over to them.

"Detectives," Victor shook Lee's hand. His voice was calm, but Lee thought he saw a flash of unease in his eyes. "What brings you here?"

"We're still looking for Olivia. What are you doing here?" Lee let an edge of accusation creep into his voice.

"I'm the manager," Victor replied. He introduced himself to Jake. "How can I help you?"

"Yesterday you said you were a bartender," Lee pressed.

"I was being modest."

"Do you know Bailey Anderson?" Jake asked.

"Yes, of course," Victor said, a flicker of something unreadable passing over his face. "He owns this bar."

"Can you tell us what he looks like?"

Victor laughed, "I've never met the man. Anderson owns this place, and several others. We communicate over email."

Jake held up the photograph of Olivia and Susan. "We need to talk about this night, Victor. New Year's Eve. Olivia and Susan were here, and you didn't mention it."

Victor's smile faltered. "I didn't think it was important."

Lee wrinkled his forehead. "You made a point of telling us that you don't cross paths with Mrs. Campbell outside the neighborhood."

Victor scratched his chin and looked off to the side. "I just meant we don't engage socially on the regular. I invite everyone I know to events here at the bar. Susan is my neighbor. That's probably why they chose to come to this party instead of one of a hundred others throughout the city."

Lee stepped forward, his eyes narrowing. "Olivia is missing, Victor. Anything could be important. Why didn't you tell us she was here?"

"I didn't remember. That was two weeks ago!"

Lee and Jake exchanged a look, silently fuming. But they needed Victor's cooperation.

"We need information about the party," Jake said, his voice measured. "Who else was there? Did you notice anything out of the ordinary?"

Victor leaned against the bar, his expression becoming more thoughtful. "It was the usual crowd. Locals, a few out-of-town folks, college kids. We have the party every year. Lots of people coming and going. I remember talking to a few regulars, but nothing unusual."

"Names, Victor," Lee pressed. "We need names of people who were here that night."

Victor nodded. "Let me think...There was Tom and Linda, they're regulars. Kevin, the bartender, might remember more people. It was just a party. Shouldn't you be looking into Olivia's boyfriend?"

"How do you know about that?" Lee squinted as his suspicion deepened.

Victor hesitated. "Uncle Jonathan told me."

Jake cleared his throat. "Your uncle told me he hadn't spoken to you in years. In fact, he didn't even know you were living in Baltimore."

Victor grimaced. "Yeah. Well, I called him yesterday after the other detectives visited. I wanted to know what was going on."

"Was he surprised?" Jake asked.

"Of course. I didn't think he was going to speak to me at all. But once I got him talking about Olivia, it all smoothed out. He told me he thought Olivia ran off with her boyfriend." Victor scratched his shoulder.

Jake showed him a picture of his sketch of Robert. "Do you recognize her boyfriend?"

"No, I've never seen him."

Lee found a picture of Marty Slye on his phone and showed it to Victor. "How about this man?"

Victor scratched his chin again, studying the photo. "Um, yeah, he does look familiar. Actually, this guy was at the New Year's party. I don't remember his name, but he was asking a lot of questions about Olivia. Kept to himself mostly. Weird guy."

Jake and Lee exchanged another look. "Why didn't you mention this before?" Jake asked, his voice rising slightly.

Victor's eyes darted. "I didn't know it was relevant. He didn't do anything suspicious, just ... asked questions."

"What kind of questions?" Lee asked.

"About Olivia. If she came here often, who she was friends with. I thought he was just a concerned friend or something," Victor said. His voice faltered a bit.

Jake sighed, slipping the photograph back into his pocket. "Is there anything else you can tell us? How often does Olivia come here?"

"Honestly, Detective, that's the only time she was here. I'd all but forgotten about it if you hadn't shown me that picture. And I'm so busy at the New Year's party ..."

"If you think of anything—" Lee pressed a business card into the bar manager's hand.

Victor's eyes darted to the side again. "Of course, detectives. I'll let you know if I remember anything else."

"So, Victor was holding out on us?" Katherine asked, taking a seat on one of the office couches.

"Not sure if it means anything." Jake sat with his fresh cup of coffee. "I'm glad we've ruled Robert out as a suspect, though."

"So am I." Robert smirked. "I hope I can help. I tried to track Olivia's cell phone location, but it's turned off or dead."

Lee stretched and headed for the water cooler. "Let me guess, the last ping was near her apartment."

"Right."

"She probably turned it off herself so you couldn't trace her," said Jake.

Katherine nodded. "Your boss said he'd get us copies of any surveillance footage your team got."

"Yeah, he told me." Robert tilted his head. "Usually we don't let civilians access that kind of thing."

Jake chuckled. "Everyone here but Sammi has top security clearances."

"Hey, where is Sammi?" Lee called from the other side of the room.

"She must be out to lunch," said Katherine. "Check for a note on my desk."

"I don't see a note." Lee stepped over to Sammi's desk. "Y'all...her computer is on. And Olivia's laptop is open. Sammi wouldn't leave them like that if she were going out for more than a couple minutes." He touched the trackpad on the laptop. "What's that password?"

Katherine opened the case folder. "Kindey44."

As soon as the profile opened, Lee slammed the lid closed. "Spyware."

Jake sprinted to Katherine's desk and hammered at the keyboard.

"What kind of spyware?" Katherine sprang to her feet.

"I recognized the program. It turns on the computer's webcam and locks it down so that the user can't shut it off."

"This was on Olivia's computer?" Robert asked as he stood.

"Hang on, guys," Jake spoke up. "Here's the security video from our office."

They looked at the monitor. A black and white image showed Sammi sitting at her desk, working on the laptop. She became frustrated and tapped at the keyboard several times. Then she got up to turn on her desktop computer.

Jake fast-forwarded the video. About ten minutes after she switched computers, Sammi looked at the door. Two men entered the room. Sammi reached for the phone. The men lunged at her, grabbing her around the waist. She tried to fight them off, but they dragged her out of the building.

With a few clicks, Jake switched to the outdoor security camera. The men carried a struggling Sammi out and shoved her into the back of a white unmarked van.

Katherine said, "Go."

23

Time slowed down as the detectives raced for the door, leaving their coats behind. Katherine was already dialing Detective Alvarez at the Baltimore PD. She leapt into her Ford, joined by Robert. Jake jumped into his Jeep, followed by Lee. The cars split up and canvassed the city, pushing the speed limit at every stretch.

Katherine swerved around larger vehicles and took corners without slowing. Robbed gripped the grab bar above the door. It didn't take long before her police scanner squawked out an APB. Sirens wailed as marked police cars joined the search.

The police scanner squawked, "Suspect vehicle spotted in the Pulaski Industrial Area, Erdman Avenue. Officers are in pursuit."

Katherine and Jake both changed course to intercept the police patrol and the kidnapper's van. The sirens grew louder as they drew closer and more police vehicles closed in. They stopped at a small warehouse with the van from the surveillance tape parked outside the building. Police cars surrounded the building as Katherine reached into the center console to grab a loaded magazine. She opened her trunk to retrieve her Glock 17 from the mounted gun safe and slid the magazine into place. Jake and Lee arrived and jumped out, weapons drawn. The three armed detectives hurried to confer with the officer in charge.

Before they could agree on a plan, a tall man in a green hooded sweatshirt came out of the warehouse, dragging Sammi in front of him. She had a gag in her mouth and was still squirming, although it was obvious she was getting tired.

The man raised a gun to the girl's head. "Get back! Get out of here or I'll kill her! I swear, I'll kill her!"

Katherine, Jake, Lee, and the police officers crouched behind the cars, weapons ready. The officer in charge spoke into a bullhorn.

"We have you surrounded! Release the girl!"

The private detectives looked at each other. This situation was getting out of control, and their friend's life was on the line. Unfortunately, the kidnapper was using Sammi as a shield. He maneuvered his human shield in front of the van.

"I'm taking the girl and leaving. Anyone follows me and she gets it!" The kidnapper opened the passenger door and backed up to the seat, pulling Sammi with him.

"I don't have a shot," Jake whispered. Katherine shook her head.

"Look...under the van." Lee pointed.

A man was shimmying across the ground under the van. As the kidnapper pulled his feet up into the passenger side, the man tapped Sammi's ankle and patted the ground.

Sammi must have understood the message, because when her captor moved to slide back into the driver's seat, Sammi fell forward, breaking his hold, and dropped to the ground. Jake fired a round at the top of the passenger door to frighten the kidnapper back as Sammi and the man shimmied farther under the van.

Katherine and police stood up and shouted, "Hands up!"

The kidnapper put up his hands and dropped his gun on the ground. Police officers rushed up to him, pulled him out of the van, and searched him.

More officers approached the warehouse door. They called for anyone inside to come out with their hands up. Katherine and Jake ran toward the shed where Sammi and the man had run, weapons still drawn.

"Hands up!" Jake shouted as they burst into the building through the side entrance.

"Katherine! Jake!" Sammi ran forward, throwing her arms around both of them as they fumbled with their guns.

Robert followed more slowly. "Quite a smart one you've got there, Mr. Mercer."

Jake holstered his gun. "You went in under the van to get her out?"

Robert nodded. "I didn't bring my service weapon to your office, so I thought I would scout around back. Turns out I got an opening to help the little lady out of a jam."

"And am I ever grateful!" Sammi beamed. "That's a bit of excitement I could have lived without."

Katherine put her gun in her belt and extended her hand to Robert. "Good work," she said by way of thanks. Peter had convinced her to consider trusting Robert. But now he'd earned her respect.

Robert smiled. "I'm as anxious as you are to find out what's going on, and why Olivia's laptop had spyware on it."

"Spyware!" Sammi covered her face. "Of course! I couldn't figure out what was going on with the laptop and then all of a sudden these big burly guys came in and…and…" She let out a big breath with a whoosh. "I think I need to sit down."

"Come on then, let's get you looked over." Katherine ushered Sammi back out to the parking lot where police officers where arresting three other men and searching the van.

"Sammi! Thank goodness you're okay." Lee threw a blanket around the girl's shoulders. "Let's get you checked out. EMTs are waiting for you."

Lee led Sammi over to the recently arrived ambulance. Jake, Katherine, and Robert made their way over to the warehouse where Police Detective Camilla Alvarez was overseeing a search.

"Hey, Cam," Katherine said.

"Kat! Jake," Detective Alvarez shook their hands. "Is Sammi okay?"

Katherine puffed air into her cheeks. "She seems okay, but I think it's just hitting her. She's with the paramedics."

"Good. I could hardly believe it when you called. Now we just need to piece together why someone would be after Sammi."

"Guys, look at this." Jake held up a computer printout of a picture of Sammi, taken from a web cam with an address written at the bottom.

"That's how they knew where to find her," Katherine said.

"Actually, they weren't after Sammi." Jake handed Katherine the photo and pointed to the top of the page.

"Secure Olivia Ames."

24

Katherine and Jake continued further into the cluttered ware-house while Detective Alvarez interviewed Robert. Papers were strewn across makeshift desks. Maps covered the walls. Shelves groaned under the weight of supplies and equipment. It was clear that the site was being used as a command center, not a warehouse.

Several BPD detectives had spread themselves throughout the warehouse, each person searching a different section. They rifled through papers, opened containers, and examined every surface for any trace of evidence to point to what the criminals were planning.

In one corner, Katherine scrutinized a wall covered in maps. She traced the lines with her finger, searching for a pattern. Jake pored over a desk covered in papers, his brow furrowed as he sifted through the jumble of documents.

"I don't see how any of this pertains to us, or Olivia." Jake went to stand beside Katherine.

"These are maps of Baltimore, Annapolis, and Washington, D.C. It must have something to do with their plan." Katherine rubbed her neck as she moved away from the maps toward the center of the room.

Boxes and crates were stacked haphazardly in the center of the room. Some were cracked open, and others were piled several layers high. Jake walked past the piles to begin searching through the mountain of papers on another desk.

Katherine slowly circled the boxes, shining her flashlight on the labels so she could read them in the dim lighting. *Cleaning supplies, rubber gloves, water bottles, zip-top bags …*

Finally, the beam fell on an object that stood out against the wood and cardboard—a blue plastic bucket. There was something about the bucket that nagged at her memory. Katherine cautiously knelt to examine the container.

The lid was ajar, as if it had been hastily abandoned. She carefully lifted the lid and peered at a mass of white crystals. Her nose twitched at the acrid stench of sulfur, and she replaced the lid and backed away. *Glad I wore gloves.*

"Fellas! Over here!" she called, waving her light.

"What you got, Kat?" Jake was the first to get to her.

"I think we've found the missing pesticide."

Detective Alvarez approached. "Find something?"

"Chlorpyrifos. A 25 kilogram tub was stolen from an agricultural processing center a few days ago. I think this might be it."

Katherine stepped aside to let the police take over. Detective Alvarez gave her team instructions before joining Katherine and Jake near the warehouse entrance.

Jake handed a stack of papers to Detective Alvarez. "I found our connection to Olivia Ames. Her first graduate research project. The title is 'The correlation between extended exposure to toxins and the probability of transplant organ rejection.' She talks about potential side effects of different common pesticides, industrial cleaners, and household chemicals. I suspect this is why they wanted to kidnap her. They got hold of this paper somehow and wanted to tap her expertise."

Detective Alvarez looked at Robert. "Were you aware of this research?"

Robert answered, "She was working on that paper when we met. I thought it was very ambitious."

"Does she mention chlorpyrifos by name?" Katherine asked.

"Yeah," Jake said. "The paper discusses the viability of organs harvested from people who have had prolonged exposure to toxins. How that exposure could damage organs and decrease the likelihood of them being accepted by the body of a trans-plant recipient. She spends a good deal of time highlighting the potential danger of choly...this pesticide and circumstances that make it even more destructive."

"You two obviously know more about what is going on here than I do," Detective Alvarez chuckled.

"We're assisting in the defense of the woman accused of stealing that tub of pesticide." Katherine pointed to the officers who had descended on the stack of boxes and the police photographer taking pictures of the plastic tub.

"Is it dangerous?"

"That much chlorpyrifos would be enough to kill 1.5 million people. Maybe more if mixed with other substances. Even if it isn't concentrated enough to kill, it can cause blindness, cancer, and other irreparable health effects." Katherine ticked the items off on her fingers.

"Considering the maps we saw and the other equipment, it

seems fairly obvious these guys were planning some kind of mass poisoning." Jake clapped Katherine on the back and grinned mischievously. "We set out to find a missing girl and wound up thwarting a bio-terrorism plot."

Katherine smirked and wiggled her eyebrow. "It was their bad luck that they took Sammi instead of Olivia."

"We've apprehended four suspects. Hopefully one of them will give us information about what is going on here," Detective Alvarez said. "We need to find out if this incident has anything to do with Olivia's disappearance."

"Doubtful," Katherine said. "They wouldn't have taken Sammi if they already had Olivia."

"There have been no reports of any unidentified victims of accidents or violent crime. Someone must be involved in her disappearance." Camilla let frustration enter her voice, "I want to talk to Olivia's father, but can't reach him."

Katherine put her fingers to her chin. "That's odd. I've been trying to talk to him, too. He was so worried, I would expect him to be calling us every day."

As Detective Alvarez left to speak with her team, Jake leaned over to whisper in Katherine's ear. "We need to move fast. If someone has Olivia, she could be in serious danger."

25

Katherine stole a glance at the young man in her passenger seat. She'd volunteered to drive Robert home while Jake went to the hospital to check on Sammi. Yesterday morning, she thought Robert was a conman after Olivia's family money. Last night, she learned he was a CIA operative and decided he was using Olivia for her intellect to further his selfish ambition.

Now he was a broken-hearted boyfriend.

And the hero who had saved Sammi's life.

Katherine gripped the steering wheel and pushed back into her seat. "Peter seems to think there is something special about you. His praise is not easy to earn."

"He's been a great mentor. He wants me to go in a different direction with my career, but he is always supportive."

"I have to admit, I was impressed with how you thought on your feet today; pulling Sammi out from under that hostile by crawling under the van." She saw the young agent smile out of the corner of her eye.

"She did most of the work herself."

"But she wouldn't have done it without help." Katherine's heart clenched when she thought about what might have happened to Sammi. "I'm grateful."

"Help me find my girl, and we'll call it even."

"I intend to do just that. And then what?"

Robert asked, "What do you mean?"

"Are you going to continue recruiting her to the Company?"

"Of course. She'd be a valuable resource."

Katherine took a deep breath as she parked at the gas station near his apartment. "Did Lee tell you what my...outburst was about the other night?"

Robert squirmed in his seat. "He said your partner was killed in action."

Katherine's voice came out so soft it wasn't even a whisper. "My partner; my husband."

Robert's eyes widened as his head snapped toward her. "I'm sorry. I didn't know."

"My husband was killed because I wasn't fast enough to save him." Tears welled up in her eyes.

Robert stayed quiet.

Katherine turned in her seat and looked directly into his eyes. "We were young, in love. We loved working together. We were the perfect team ... And now he's dead. Before you decide to pull your sweetheart into your world ... this dark, oppressively evil world, will you be able to live with the guilt of knowing that you are responsible for whatever trouble comes for her."

Robert took a breath and looked away. "I try not to look too deeply into the darkness that lurks in my job."

"That's when bad things happen—when you aren't looking. And something will happen. My parents were shot when their covers were compromised. My husband was blown up when a mission went sideways. And I'm an emotional wreck with a guilt complex. No one comes out unscathed. And no matter what you tell yourself, you cannot protect her. Look at what happened to Sammi. That was meant for Olivia. If it had been your heart in that man's arms, would you still have had the presence of mind to react as you did? Or would it have been a different ending?"

Robert said, "Olivia is such a bright, beautiful woman, with so much to offer."

"I'm not arguing that. My question is, have you and she considered where her light can shine brightest? Is it worth the risk for the darkness to snuff out her light? Will everything she has to offer shine best in the shadows of the intelligence community, or on the stage of medical research and advancement in the private sector? I'm also saying that if you love her, you must let it be her decision. You set out to recruit her, but trust me, if you force her to make a choice that is not her own and it goes badly, you will never be able to forgive yourself."

They sat in silence for a long minute. "Thank you, Ms. Carson. I will give your advice some serious thought. And thank you for working so hard to find Olivia."

"I know you fought with Olivia in the library, Gordon." Katherine kept her tone professional but gentle. She could see the stress etched on his face and wanted to ease him into recounting the events.

Gordon took a deep breath and began, "I went to the library to return some books. Olivia was alone at the front desk. We've had disagreements, but this time ... I lost my temper."

Katherine had located Gordon in the musty office that graduate students used for their studies. The desk between them was piled high with lab reports, highlighting the academic pressure the student faced.

"What sparked the argument?" Katherine asked.

"It was about the research grant," Gordon replied, frustration creeping into his voice. "I was mad because Olivia is being considered first, even though I applied before she did and have been working on it longer. I told her it wasn't fair."

"And what did she say?" Katherine prompted.

"She said she didn't even know I had applied."

"Was that true?"

Gordon furrowed his brow. "It's a competitive field, and I'm not obligated to share my plans with her. I told her that, and things started to escalate."

"How did they escalate?" Katherine asked, noting Gordon's arrogance clouded his logic.

"Olivia suggested we could have applied jointly," Gordon said, shaking his head. "I scoffed at the idea. I told her that her approach to scaffolding the tissue is too traditional. We need to innovate if we want to stand out."

"How did she respond to that?"

"She said the grant application board must agree with her." Bitterness crept into Gordon's voice. "She said my methods are risky and unproven, and it's not worth wasting time on something that might not work. But she has time to sit around and stick cloves into oranges. She's such a goody two shoes! "

Katherine leaned in. "What happened next?"

Gordon avoided Katherine's gaze. "That's when things got heated. I raised my voice. I told her she always gets more attention from Dr. Mahoney. I accused her of sabotaging my experiments by hogging lab resources."

"And did she?" Katherine asked, her eyes steady on his face.

Gordon shook his head. "Look, we're both under a lot of pressure. The competition is fierce, and the stakes are high."

Katherine leaned back in her chair, studying him for a moment. "Gordon, I need you to be honest with me. Is there any-thing else I should know? Any other conflicts or issues between you and Olivia?"

Gordon sighed, running a hand through his hair. "We have clashed before. But it's all been professional. This argument ... it just got out of hand."

Katherine considered the young man and wondered how far out of hand the argument had gone. She asked quietly, "Do you know where Olivia is now?"

Gordon drew himself up and squared his shoulders, "Is that an accusation?"

"No." Katherine often didn't need to prompt someone to unravel their own story.

"I didn't have anything to do with Olivia going missing. I admit I lost my temper with her, but the last time I saw her, she was very much alive and well."

"When was that?"

"Friday."

Katherine narrowed her eyes. "Yesterday, you told me you hadn't seen her since lab on Tuesday."

Gordon stiffened. "Oh, I thought you meant when I had last talked to her. I just saw her in passing on Friday."

"Where?"

"She was on her way into the Bio-med building for the meet-up." He picked at a hangnail.

"Dr. Mahoney told me that Olivia didn't go to the meet-up on Friday."

"Well, she must have changed her mind. She was going into the building. Look, I have to be somewhere. I didn't do anything to Olivia, and I can't tell you anything else."

"Gordon," Katherine called. "Do you know a man named Bailey Anderson?"

He paused and turned, "No."

"What about Marty Slye, a private detective."

"No. Any more questions?"

Katherine waved him away and the student stormed off. She had a lot more questions, but none she thought the student could—or would—answer.

26

"Hello, this is Katherine Carson. May I speak to Mr. Ames?"

"I'm sorry, Mr. Ames is in conference and can't be disturbed. May I take a message?"

"Yes, ma'am. Please ask him to call me as soon as he is free. He has my number."

"Yes, Ms. Carson. I will give him the message."

Katherine hung up the phone and gripped the steering wheel. She was sitting in her car in a parking lot across from a Wells Fargo Bank. Gordon's argument with Olivia and his deceptive answers made him a strong suspect. So, after giving the student a head start, Katherine followed him.

Gordon left the bank and walked briskly to his car. Katherine started her engine, merging into traffic a safe distance behind him. They drove through the bustling city streets until Gordon parked beside a bar.

Katherine parked farther down the street, approaching the bar on foot. She stopped short at the corner of the building next door. Gordon hadn't gone inside. Instead, he was standing in the alley behind the bar with two other figures. She arranged her scarf to distort her face and shuffled toward the front of the bar. The figures in the alley paid no attention to her, but Katherine noticed a quick exchange of parcels.

She paused when she rounded the corner of the bar. Jonathan Ames' nephew Victor stood on the sidewalk beside a battered gray Oldsmobile. He was talking to a woman whose pale skin and frizzy blonde hair matched his own.

Victor pasted on a wide smile as Katherine approached them. "Detective Katherine! How charming to see you again. How goes the search for Olivia?"

The woman beside him stiffened, her gaze fixed on the detective. Victor patted her arm and explained, "I was just telling my sister the sad news."

"Your sister? How nice to meet you," Katherine said, keeping one eye on the alley's only exit.

"Vera, this is Detective Katherine Carson. She and her team are searching for dear Olivia." Victor gave his sister a gentle nudge, and she stuck out her hand to limply hold Katherine's.

"What brings you here, Detective?" Vera asked.

As much as Katherine wanted to ask the siblings about their cousin, at that moment Gordon exited the alley and circled to the front of the building. "Victor, that young man entering the bar." She jerked her chin.

Victor looked at the door and nodded. "Gordon. He's a student at Johns Hopkins too."

"Then he's a regular?" Katherine heard the muffled music become clear as Gordon opened the door.

Victor looked back at the detective when Gordon disappeared inside. "Oh, yes. He's here all the time."

The other two figures slinked out of the alley and hurried away from them.

"What about those guys?" Katherine asked.

Victor's expression darkened. "They're local pushers. I've called the cops on them before, but they've yet to be caught."

Katherine crossed her arms. "Looks like Gordon must be buying drugs."

"That's a shame," Victor said, shaking his head. "He seems like a bright young man."

"Have you ever noticed any suspicious behavior from him? Or hanging around Olivia?"

"Olivia was only here that one time, I'm sure. I realize I should have mentioned it the first time we spoke, but it honestly didn't occur to me. Gordon comes on a regular basis, and others from JHU as well, especially the older students. We're not a college bar, really, but it's close by and I think they like getting away from the college crowd."

Vera squeezed her brother's arm and cleared her throat. "I should be going," she murmured.

"Of course, dear!" Victor patted her shoulder. "Thanks for stopping by. Detective, did you want to come inside and warm up? You can talk to Gordon."

"No, thank you, I don't want to tip my hand just yet. I need to be going as well." Katherine turned to walk back to her car as Victor hurried into the bar.

When she heard classic rock music ring clear, she turned back. Victor had gone inside, but Vera was waiting for street traffic to slow before climbing into her driver's seat.

Katherine hurried to the car and rapped on the passenger window. Vera's pale face went sallow as she looked out at the detective. Katherine motioned for her to roll the window down. Vera leaned across the seat to manually crank down the window, knocking the contents of a purple bag onto the floor.

"Oh! Can I help you, Ms. Ames?" Katherine offered.

"No, no, I have it," Vera said as she grabbed a hairdryer and set of combs to stuff back into the bag.

"Okay. Would you mind answering a few questions for me?"

"I really must be going. I have to pick up a friend from work." She continued picking up bobby pins and other accessories while Katherine spoke.

"How well do you know Olivia? I was under the impression your side of the family didn't keep in touch with them."

"Oh, that's old news. Of course we were upset when we lost the family fortune. But Olivia is still family! I follow her on Facebook, keep up with what she's doing. She's a sweet girl."

"Ms. Ames, if you have any information you can give us, anything at all, it could help us locate your cousin."

"No, I'm afraid I don't. Are you close to finding Olivia?" Vera looked up with genuine concern evident in her features.

"We're doing all we can." Katherine handed Vera one of her business cards. "Please contact me if you can think of anything."

Vera dropped the card into the bag and rolled the window back up. "Yes, okay. Excuse me, I'm running late." She revved the old engine and pulled away, tires screeching.

Katherine sighed as she walked back to her own car. Vera's question echoed in her mind. "Are you close to finding Olivia?"

As Katherine started her engine, her BlackBerry rang with a phone call from Lee.

"The FBI has detained the man they believe is using the name Bailey Anderson."

"That's great news!" Katherine smiled. *Maybe this lead will pan out after all.*

"The man is Jonathan Ames."

27

Katherine and Lee were standing outside an interview room with Ted Davis. Mr. Ames sat uncomfortably on the other side of the glass. He didn't look like the same man who had spoken to Katherine on Monday morning. His haggard face hadn't been shaved in a couple of days. His hair was unruly, and his eyes had lost their confident sparkle.

"I appreciate you giving us this opportunity, Ted," Lee shook the agent's hand.

"I owe you for finding the Anderson lead in the first place. I'm also hoping that one of you will be able to get through to him if you talk about your case with his daughter. He hasn't said anything since we brought him in."

"Does he have a lawyer?" Katherine asked quietly.

"I'm sure he has an army of them, but he's refused to call one," the agent said.

"I'd like to speak with him alone, if I may," she requested.

"That's fine, no evidence that he's violent. Of course, we'll be watching from here."

Katherine bit the inside of her cheek and made her way to the door. Mr. Ames looked up when she entered the room, but didn't speak. Katherine's mind rehearsed possibilities as she settled into a chair opposite him.

"What happened, Jonathan?"

Silence.

Ted had told them what happened. They had staked out Anderson's apartment, leaving everything as they'd found it. Last night, at about 11:30 pm, Jonathan Ames had arrived at the apartment building. He went directly to the Anderson apartment and let himself in with a key. Then he went to the desk, opened the laptop, and typed in the password to unlock it. The password that the FBI technicians had been unable to crack.

Katherine took a deep breath. "They say Bailey Anderson has been milking your company for six years. They've found forged employee records. Inflated salaries. Hundreds of fraudulent transactions traceable to a device owned by Bailey Anderson."

Mr. Ames shifted in his seat and looked at his hands. He kept his mouth closed.

Ted had told them that Mr. Ames had opened the company's payroll software and started to schedule another series of trans-actions. Exact replicas of the fraudulent ones they'd discovered. He didn't have an alibi for any of the previous transactions. He had a key to the apartment, and the password to the computer. It didn't look good.

"Bailey Anderson also hired a private detective named Marty Slye to follow Olivia and report on her activities. He told Marty that he worked for Ames Enterprises."

Mr. Ames face flushed, but he didn't move or speak.

The FBI had also confirmed Olivia and Jonathan Ames' banking details with the Baltimore Police Department. When Jonathan was found, he had been attempting to schedule payments directly to his daughter's bank account.

Sloppy, yes.

But in Ted's words, "Criminals always make mistakes. That's how they get caught." They'd cleared the CEO in their initial investigation. *But now he's tied to a fictitious employee whom no one has ever seen.*

Katherine leaned forward. "I think I know what's going on," she whispered. "But I can't help you if you don't talk to me."

Jonathan Ames finally looked up to meet her eyes. He whispered back, "Are you close to finding Olivia?"

It was all the confirmation Katherine needed.

Katherine finds herself standing on a long dirt road. Ahead of her is an old-fashioned farmhouse with a palm tree in the front yard. Katherine walks toward the farmhouse and up to the front door. She reaches to open the door, but the doorknob is missing. She turns to leave, but hears a gunshot from inside. She throws all her body weight against the door and forces it open.

The house is eerily empty of any furnishings. She goes to a door in the center of the house and opens it. Looking down into the darkness, she hears muffled moans then a scream. Katherine pulls her knife out of her pocket and opens it, moving cautiously down the dark staircase.

At the bottom of the stairs, she finds a dark room. A blonde-headed woman is huddled on a couch, her back to the staircase.

Seeing no other people in the room, Katherine moves toward her. She places a hand on the woman's shoulder. The woman turns slowly.

Katherine's heart stops when she sees the face of her dead husband, Daniel, with blood streaming down his forehead.

"Run."

Daniel speaks, and Katherine runs. She takes the stairs two at a time, but the staircase grows longer and longer with every step she takes, and Daniel's voice becomes increasingly urgent as he yells, "Run! Run!"

She runs so hard she loses her breath and the muscles in her legs burn. Suddenly, the door at the top of the endless staircase flies open, and a man's figure throws the lifeless body of Olivia Ames down the stairs. Katherine ducks and looks behind her. At the foot of the stairs, Olivia lands atop a gruesome pile—the corpses of Katherine's parents, her husband, friends, and partners killed in the line of duty.

Katherine sat bolt upright in bed, her body drenched in sweat. Her heart pounded loudly in her ears, her breathing was labored, and every muscle in her arms and legs cried out in pain. She hadn't had a nightmare that real in a very long time.

She scanned her bedroom for her touchstones—a salt lamp, an old-fashioned clock, the painting of a white tiger. Remember-ing the meaning behind each familiar object calmed her heart.

This case was no longer a missing persons case. It was a rescue mission. She would not let Olivia be added to the pile of bodies in her past. She had failed to save Daniel. She could not fail again.

28

"We spent hours yesterday going through the CIA's surveillance footage," Jake said as he stretched out on a couch. "We didn't find anything useful. We spotted Marty a few more times, but nothing else. And they got no footage at all for Friday when she went missing."

"Buenos Dias, everyone."

"Sammi!" Everyone stood up and clapped as their young colleague entered the room.

"Good morning, Sammi!" Katherine pulled her into a gentle hug. "I'm so glad you're feeling okay."

"I am. Thanks for letting me come in to the office. I want to help finish this case."

"Absolutely. Since the doctor cleared you, there's no reason you can't work."

Sammi hung up her coat and gave both Jake and Lee a hug. A sharp rap on the door caused everyone to look up. A woman with dark curls and porcelain skin, dressed smartly in a brown suit and red blouse, entered the room.

"Maggie, come in!" Jake beamed and took the coat that was draped over her arm.

"Hi, all. Jake." Margaret waved to the room and dipped her head coyly in Jake's direction.

"Professor Mitchell!" Sammi smiled. "Want some coffee?"

"Not right now, hon. I'm sure glad you weren't injured in your ordeal." Margaret sat gracefully on the sofa nearest the door without removing her coat. "I just came to fill you all in on the direction my case has taken."

Jake sat on the other couch as far away from Margaret as possible. Katherine and Lee looked at each other and rolled their eyes slightly before sitting down.

The lawyer continued. "First of all, I appreciate you all getting a statement from the construction witness. But now, that's icing on the cake to prove my client isn't guilty."

"Evidence from the warehouse?" Katherine asked.

Margaret accepted a steaming cup of coffee from Sammi before responding. "That's right. That tub you found was indeed the stolen container of chlorpyrifos. My client had nothing to do with the theft. From what I've gathered from the police, the men who took Sammi were part of some kind of eco-terrorist group. They wanted information from Olivia."

"What kind of information?" Lee asked.

"Olivia had done extensive research on this particular pesticide. Apparently, it's the most common pesticide in the United States, even though breathing or ingesting it can cause serious side effects ranging from blurred vision and headaches to seizures, coma, and death." Margaret shook her head.

Lee made a face. "Sounds like nasty stuff."

"It is," Katherine and Margaret said at the same time.

"Could the stolen pesticide have anything to do with Olivia being missing?" Sammi asked.

"No, the terrorists had no idea who Olivia was, just her name on a research paper," said Margaret.

"How did they get their hands on that?" asked Katherine.

"Allegedly a student named Ivan Rosen sold it to them."

Jake grunted. Katherine knew how he felt about terrorists and shared his revulsion.

Margaret continued. "So, the terrorists found a way to steal the container. And they had a copy of this paper which led them to believe Olivia could help them expose people to pesticides in a way to cause maximum damage."

"Why would they do that?" Sammi asked.

Katherine put her hand on her assistant's shoulder. "People have all kinds of motives for the bad things they do."

Jake nearly growled, "Eco-terror groups tend to target organizations that they think are hurting the environment."

"By hurting people?" Sammi's eyes were wide.

"No it doesn't," Margaret agreed. "The FBI will sort out all of that. The important thing for me is that my client is vindicated."

Lee stretched his neck. "I wonder why Rosen sold them the paper in the first place. Just for the money?"

Katherine said, "I doubt it. I suspect he had darker motives. He as much as said that destroying people's faith in human organ donors would result in more government funding."

"So, if they were really after Olivia, why did they kidnap me?" asked Sammi.

"Mr. Ames took Olivia's computer to a repair shop. That part is a little fuzzy, because they had to have another contact, someone who knew Olivia needed her laptop repaired."

"That could have been Ivan too," said Katherine.

"However they knew, they found out where the Ames' get computer repair work done and had someone there to install the spyware. Then they sent an email which would trigger the program when opened." Margaret got up from the couch and helped herself to another cup of coffee.

Sammi put her hands on her head. "Oh! I opened all her emails since she went missing looking for leads."

"One of them allowed them to access the computer's location and webcam. They got a picture of you from a screen grab. Then gave the picture to their thugs and waited for you to power on again to confirm your location and that you were there with the computer." Katherine went to the cabinets near the sink and found a to-go lid for her friend.

"Wow, I'm glad you guys followed me."

"Us, too." Jake said.

Margaret finished stirring her coffee before putting on the lid. "Well, gang, I'd better get to the office."

Katherine gave her a quick hug and said, "Thanks for the update, Mags. Let us know if there's anything else you need."

Margaret giggled and waggled her fingers in Jake's direction. "You know I will, hon. See you!"

Katherine broke out into a big open smile and had to turn away from Jake to keep it hidden. She picked up the office phone when it rang.

"Carson Investigations. This is Katherine."

"Hello, Detective, how is the investigation?"

"Ms. Nichols," Katherine raised her voice and her eyebrows, "how nice to hear from you." Jake, Lee, and Sammi quieted down and watched her.

"Have you found Olivia?"

"No, not yet." Katherine tucked the cordless phone between her ear and shoulder so she could get herself a cup of water.

"Did you find anything useful in the books?"

"No, I can't say that we did."

"Really? I was so sure that some of those names or numbers would be important."

"Names? Numbers?" Katherine put her cup down and waved to get her colleagues' attention.

"In the books, dear! You did go through all of them, didn't you?"

Katherine wrinkled her forehead and pointed at the stack of books. "No, we haven't been through all of them yet.

"Well, I'm sure that there is something in there that will help you. Let me know if you find out anything."

"Thank you, Ms.—" Katherine looked at the phone in disbelief as the woman on the other end hung up.

"Miss Marple says the clues are in the books." Katherine placed the phone back in its cradle.

"I thought she said the evidence was the books, not in the books," said Lee. He got up and went to counter where the books had been sitting since Tuesday.

"I think she did. Apparently, she thought we'd figure it out for ourselves."

Lee stuck his tongue out and grudgingly started flipping through one of the library books.

Jake asked, "So, Kat, do you believe what the FBI is saying about Jonathan Ames?"

"Not at all. In fact, I think it proves that Olivia has been kidnapped, and we need to redouble our efforts to find her.

Unfortunately, now that her father is a suspect, the police won't be helping us anymore."

"Hey, guys?"

They all looked over at Lee who was holding up one of the library books.

"Looks like there really could be clues in these." He turned the book so the pages faced them. They could clearly see a bright pink square and a yellow square of paper stuck to the pages. "We may have Olivia's notes."

29

Half an hour later, colorful sticky notes covered the coffee table. Yellow squares had quotes from the books probably to be included in a future research paper. Green squares had the names of authors and titles of books or academic papers for reference later. Pink squares had brief notes such as "increased capacity," "genetic predisposition," and "relevant bio-markers."

There were only four blue post-it notes in the whole stack of books. One of them was a grocery list. The other three were phone numbers.

The first phone number belonged to a hospital in Washington, DC. Olivia had interviewed one of their teaching doctors for her research paper.

The second number belonged to the Cut Right Salon where they'd visited a couple days ago.

Lee called the last number and heard, "The voicemail box for this user is not set up."

He put his hands behind his head and leaned back in his

chair. "That felt like I was back in DC."

Katherine knew it was code for, "What a waste of time."

Sammi said, "You never throw away research ... I don't believe Olivia would return these books with the notes still inside."

"So, you think someone else put the books in the book drop?" asked Jake.

"That's what Ms. Nichols thought too." Katherine shrugged.

Sammi asked, "Can one of you get your police friends to find out who owns that number?"

Katherine shook her head. "I can ask, but it wouldn't help unless they happen to recognize it. The police would need probable cause to get records from a cell phone company."

Sammi nodded as she went to her desk and began working on the computer.

"Speaking of cell phones," Lee said as his rang. He answered. "Hello?"

"Hi, I just had a missed call from this number."

"Yes, I was calling to find out if you know an Olivia Ames."

"Olivia? Sure, I know her."

"My name is Lee Stewart. I'm a private detective. Would you mind if I put you on speaker so my colleagues can hear you?"

"I guess so. A private detective? What's going on?"

Lee quickly hit the speakerphone button. "Before I answer that, would you mind if I ask what your name is?"

"I'm Susan Campbell. How did you get my number?"

Katherine jumped in to answer. "Ms. Campbell, I'm Katherine Carson, another detective. We found your phone number on a sticky note belonging to Olivia."

"What's going on? Is Olivia okay?" Susan's voice began to sound shaky.

"Olivia has gone missing. No one has seen or heard from her this week. We're trying to find out where she is."

"Missing! No, I just saw her Friday afternoon!"

"We know. But Friday evening, Olivia told her father she was going to study all weekend at home. On Saturday, she wasn't at her apartment and wouldn't answer her phone. Her father hired us to find out where she is," Katherine explained.

"Gosh. I can't believe it. I hope she's okay."

"Can you tell me, Ms. Campbell, if there was anything unusual about Olivia's behavior on Friday?" asked Lee.

"No! She seemed fine. She was a little miffed at her boyfriend because they'd been in an argument. But she'd pretty much moved past it by the time I saw her. She was too excited about her new hairstyle."

"Why did she want a new look?" Katherine asked, "Was she planning something special?"

"No, it was my idea. She has such gorgeous hair, I wanted to do something different with it, just for fun. I hope that's not what got her in trouble!"

"What do you mean?"

"Well, you know, you hear about killers who target specific profiles of women. I made her blonde ... I hope that some psycho didn't kidnap her because of her blonde hair."

Lee rolled his eyes dramatically, looking to the ceiling.

Katherine stifled a laugh and raised her brows. *Stranger things have happened.*

"Is there anything else you can tell me about Friday?" she asked.

"Well, Olivia did pack up my stylist tools. I was running late to meet my husband. We're on a cruise this week. She was going to keep them for me and get them back to me next week when we get back home."

Lee jumped in. "Were these tools in a big purple tote bag? Kind of square with lots of pockets?"

"Yeah, that's mine. Did you find it?"

"It was in the back of Olivia's car."

Katherine knit her brows and pursed her lips. "Ms. Campbell, do you know a woman named Vera?"

"Well, sure. My mom's name is Vera. But she hasn't gone by that in years. She goes by Megan Russell."

Lee and Katherine looked at each other with eyes wide.

"When did she change her name?"

"Oh, nearly 30 years ago when she and Dad got married. She dropped her first name and kept the middle one. She never liked the name Vera."

"Did your mom know Olivia well? We found a photo of you at a New Year's Party."

"Oh, yeah! They met a couple weeks ago at the party at Uncle Victor's bar."

"Your Uncle Victor's bar?" Katherine let her mouth hang open and looked at Jake, who threw his hands out in a gesture of bewilderment.

Susan laughed. "We had a great time. Uncle Victor invited us all to the New Year's Party so they could meet Olivia."

"It's great when families can get along." Katherine wanted to hear more, but she didn't want to scare her away by asking too many questions.

"Yeah. I was worried at first. Growing up, I grew up hearing about this big family feud. Then one day, Olivia finds me on Facebook, we meet up, and we get along. We kept our friendship secret for a long time, but somehow Uncle Victor found out and told my mom."

"Oh, how did that go?"

"At first Mom was mad, but after she talked it over with Uncle Victor, they asked if they could meet her. I knew Olivia wanted to be more connected to family, so I said sure. The New Year's party was a blast."

"Can you tell me—"

"Hey, so sorry to cut you off, but we've got to get back on the ship. I won't have cell service again till Sunday, but please, do keep me updated."

The blast of a ship's horn half covered Katherine's farewell as the call ended.

Lee grabbed his phone and pulled up the pictures he'd taken of Olivia's car the first day. He swiped through the photos and showed Katherine the stylist's tote bag.

"I saw this tote bag in Vera Ames' car." Katherine was certain.

"It can't be the same. Maybe mother and daughter have matching bags?" Lee handed his phone to Jake.

Katherine shook her head. "I'm sure it's the same bag I saw."

"But how did she get it out of Olivia's car?" Lee asked. "I kept the spare car key I found so no one else would be able to get in."

"Is there any way it could have been Vera Megan that Ms. Nichols saw on Friday night?" Sammi asked from her desk.

Lee smirked. "I suspect that Ms. Nichols has no trouble telling the difference between a man and a woman."

Jake jumped in, "But it could have been Victor. He hid the fact that Susan Campbell is his niece."

The pieces of the puzzle were starting to click into place, but Katherine didn't want to jump to conclusions. "Sammi, research Vera Megan Ames Russell. Jake, track down Marty Slye and show him a picture of Victor. Lee, trace Victor's employment history. And give me the spare keys to Olivia's car."

Jake grabbed his coat while Lee found the key where he'd put it in a desk drawer.

Katherine took the key and picked up her own jacket. "I'm going back to Olivia's apartment. I want to see for myself if that bag is still there."

Katherine circled Olivia's car. The backseat was empty. The bag of hairstyling tools was gone. There were no signs of forced entry on the car. Whoever took the bag must have a key. Katherine's phone rang. It was Sammi.

"Now that we've got a full name and phone number, I was able to get a little more information on Vera Megan. I found the obituary of her husband a couple years ago. He was a bigwig at a local accounting firm. Vera Megan must be living off insurance, because she doesn't have a job. I haven't found a home address, but I'll keep looking."

Lee's voice came on the line next, "Victor is the manager at Bailey's Bar. But his lifestyle far exceeds what his salary should allow. And he has no debts. He must have a secret income."

Katherine called Jake. "Did you find Marty?"

"He's right here," Jake answered. "And you were right. He's identified Victor Ames as his client."

30

"Why wouldn't Mr. Ames tell us if he thought Olivia was kidnapped?" Jake drummed his hands on his knees. "He seemed so confident it was Robert

"I think he was convinced of that because Victor bungled the initial ransom note." Katherine was chewing her bottom lip. The case was coming together, but Olivia might be running out of time. "Victor has been using the identity of Bailey Anderson to get the money he thinks he deserves from his uncle. He started with a scheme to bilk the company, but when the fraud was uncovered, he needed a new plan. He hired Marty to spy on Olivia, and found out that his niece Susan was friendly with her."

"Susan mentioned, 'Uncle Victor found out somehow,'" Lee pointed out.

"It doesn't explain why Mr. Ames isn't talking," Jake argued.

Katherine paced the room. "It doesn't explain a lot of things, but I suspect this wasn't a straightforward ransom demand."

"Guys! I got it!" Sammi jumped up from her computer and

ran over to the group. "I dug up Susan's wedding announcement in the Baltimore Sun archives. The proud parents are listed along with their address for congratulations."

Katherine took the piece of paper Sammi offered. "This is out near the state park. This is where they're holding her." Her intuition was on fire.

"Hang on, Kat, you're way ahead of us," Lee said.

"Guys, Victor admitted to you he talked to Jonathan Ames after we visited him. What if he called to give his uncle insttructions that would frame him as Bailey Anderson."

Jake and Lee looked at each other. Jake nodded slowly. "If Jonathan believed Olivia's life was in danger, he wouldn't hesitate to follow any instructions he was given."

"And he wouldn't talk," Lee finished. "What about Vera?"

Katherine continued, "She was nervous when we talked on the phone, timid in person. She didn't mastermind this plan. But she must have had the keys to Olivia's car, or she couldn't have gotten Susan's bag out of the back seat. I bet she'd do whatever her brother told her to. And you said it yourself, Lee, Victor clearly had a secret source of income."

"Vera could be living off that income too." Sammi offered, clearly convinced by Katherine's theory. "Should I call the police?"

"Yes, call Camilla and give her an update." Katherine got up and put on her coat.

Jake shook his head. "No judge will give her a warrant with the evidence we've got."

"No. And we aren't waiting for the police. We have to do this now. Olivia could be in danger." Katherine strapped an empty holster to her side. "Give Camilla the address and tell her that we're going there to look for Olivia."

"Right!" Sammi said.

Jake and Lee followed Katherine outside.

"Jake, you drive." Katherine loaded and holstered the Glock she kept locked in her trunk. Then she climbed into the front seat of Jake's Jeep. The tension rose as Jake navigated the narrow streets north of the city.

The city faded from view, and structures became fewer and farther apart. Arriving at the address, they saw a crumbling farmhouse-style home. Jake drove past and parked near the trees at the side of the road, out of view of the house.

Katherine and Lee followed Jake as he made his way up the tree line. When they got close to the house, Jake motioned for Lee to circle around behind it. Katherine and Jake approached the front of the house, crouching as they passed below the window. Katherine paused when she heard a woman's voice yelling, "Where is she? What have you done with her?"

Katherine swatted Jake's arm and motioned for him to wait. She clung to the wall and slowly slid up to look in the window from an angle to avoid being seen.

Katherine could just make out Victor Ames sitting at a breakfast table, banging it with his fist. The person he was yelling at was out of sight.

"We have to make him pay!"

"You promised me you wouldn't hurt her!" Vera stepped into view, her hands clutched to her chest.

Victor jumped up from his seat and grabbed his sister by the shoulders, shaking her violently. "You will do as I say—"

Katherine didn't wait any longer. She pulled her gun out of its holster and Jake followed suit. Together they ran to the front door and kicked it in. Their movements were synchronized from years of practice as Jake stood tall and Katherine crouched low.

"Freeze!"

Vera screamed. Victor threw her to the floor and tried to run for the back door. Lee burst in before he could escape. Katherine knelt beside Vera who was unconscious after hitting her head on a chair. Jake helped Lee wrestle Victor back into the room and held him face-first against the wall.

"Watch them both and call 911." Katherine said, nodding to Lee. She and Jake retraced their steps to the front door and searched the house.

At the back of the living room, Katherine opened a narrow door. Her heart pounded as the dimly lit stairs beckoned her downward. She descended carefully, each step creaking under her weight.

At the bottom, she found a small room, empty except for a couch draped in mussed bedsheets. The air was thick with the scent of mold and mildew. Her eyes scanned the room quickly.

Katherine's pulse quickened as she raced back up the stairs. Bursting into the living room, she found Victor sitting hand-cuffed in a chair.

Her voice cracked with desperation as she repeated Vera's plea, "Where is she? What have you done with her?"

Victor leaned forward, a smug smile playing on his lips. "I don't know what you mean, detective."

Katherine clenched her fists, her mind racing.

This is far from over.

31

Detective Camilla Alvarez sat in a police interrogation room across the table from Vera Megan Ames Russell. Katherine and Jake watched through a one-way mirror.

"Mrs. Russell, tell me what happened," Detective Alvarez asked.

"It wasn't my fault, it was all my brother's idea." The woman's round face was pink and splotchy from crying. Detective Alvarez handed her a packet of tissues. Vera blew her nose.

"Tell me what happened."

"Victor has been working at Uncle Johnny's company…"

"Ames Enterprises."

"Yes. He's been working there and trying to get money some-how. I don't know much about business, but he's been taking care of me for years."

"How did Olivia fit into his plan?"

"Well, she didn't. Not at first. But last fall…" Vera wiped her eyes and shook her head.

"What happened last fall?" the detective prompted.

Vera sighed. "He said that Uncle Johnny fired him. Victor was so angry." She touched the bandage on her head.

Katherine recognized fear in the other woman's face. "I don't think that's the first time Victor attacked his sister."

"No," Jake answered.

"It won't really be kidnapping, dear sister," Victor coaxed. "It will be like a family vacation retreat at your house, from which she may not leave until her bill is paid."

"My house?" Vera asked in a shaky voice.

"Yes, of course, dear sister, I couldn't very well keep her in my home, could I? You wouldn't want Susan involved, would you?"

Vera bit her lip and shook her head. She hated that Victor lived next door to her daughter.

"But you are so far away from town that if she were to become suspicious, no one would be able to hear her yell."

Vera nodded.

Victor sneered, that face that made her skin crawl. "Good. Then, we will invite Olivia over for dinner at your house. We'll do it while Susan and Douglas are out of town, that should make you happy."

Vera simpered, "Thank you, Victor."

"Of course, we'll tell Olivia she has to keep it secret. We wouldn't want to upset her father."

"You won't hurt her, will you, Victor?" Vera unconsciously rubbed her right arm, which her brother had broken many times over the years.

Victor's smile softened, "Of course not. We just need enough money to help us get by until I find another job."

"Won't we be arrested?"

"Are you kidding? The rich brat's gonna have had an adventure. Uncle Johnny will be so happy to get his precious girl back that he won't bother pressing charges. And if he does, we'll tell them she came willingly and we thought she wanted to stay. It will be her word against ours."

Victor lounged in the metal chair, a smug smile tugging at the corners of his mouth. Katherine's skin crawled. His arrogance was infuriating. She'd been watching for over an hour as Detective Alvarez questioned him, trying to break through his facade.

Detective Alvarez leaned forward. "We need to know where Olivia is, Victor. This isn't a game."

Victor shrugged, his expression unchanged. "I don't know what you're talking about."

"Your sister has already told us everything," Detective Alvarez pressed. "She's implicated you in the kidnapping."

Victor's eyes flickered briefly, but he quickly regained his composure. "My sister is a liar. She always has been."

Detective Alvarez stood up, pacing the small room. "You're not walking out of here, Victor. Not until we get the truth."

He chuckled softly, the sound sending a shiver down Katherine's spine. "Good luck with that, detective. You have nothing on me."

Detective Alvarez stormed out. She joined Katherine in the observation room.

"I believe everything you said about him, Kat," she said. "But it's not enough. We don't even have hard evidence that a kidnapping occurred, let alone that he did it. Vera implicated him, but it's his word against hers. It's not enough to even get a search warrant."

Katherine sighed heavily. "Lee is with the FBI. Jonathan Ames refuses to cooperate unless we've found Olivia first."

Lightning flashed in Detective Alvarez's eyes, "That's what this creep is counting on. You have to find her, Kat. My hands are tied. Vera doesn't know what happened to Olivia. The last time she saw her, she was sleeping on the couch in the basement. I'll keep putting the heat on Victor, but I don't think he'll crack in time."

Katherine pressed her lips into a firm line. She stared at Victor through the one-way glass, taking in every detail of his body language, his attitude, and his demeanor. If they were going to find their missing woman, she needed to crawl inside his skin. Olivia's life depended on it.

"His place is immaculate," Jake said, tapping the steering wheel. "No signs of any financial fraud or kidnapping."

"Outside his expensive taste in home furnishings," Katherine muttered. She watched police headquarters fade into the background as Jake pulled away.

"It's no crime to enjoy luxury. But his bar manager's salary is supposedly his only income stream."

Katherine clenched her fists, trying to keep her frustration in check. "My instinct says Olivia is somewhere on the farm. We have to go back."

Jake nodded as he headed back toward Vera's house. Katherine felt the tension rising as they arrived at the farmhouse for the second time. They searched the house even more thoroughly this time. Every room, every closet, every hidden corner.

When they reached the basement, they scanned the entire space with their flashlights. The single bulb in one corner was barely enough to light the stairs.

Jake shined his flashlight along the floor, looking for irregularities. Katherine tapped the walls. Finally, her hand hit against a section of the wall that sounded different. She pushed against it, and they heard a soft metallic click.

Jake rushed to help her pry the hidden door open. Behind the door, a narrow staircase led down to a hidden cellar. Looking down into the darkness, Katherine heard muffled moans.

"Olivia!" Katherine called out, rushing down the stairs with Jake close behind. In the dim light of their flashlights, they saw her huddled in a corner, looking weak and terrified.

Katherine knelt beside her, checking her pulse. Her eyes were dilated and her skin was cool to the touch. Katherine pulled off her coat and wrapped it around the young woman. "We found you, Olivia. You're safe now."

Jake pulled out his phone and dialed 911, urgency in his voice. "We need an ambulance immediately. We found Olivia Ames. She's in bad shape."

Jake put his coat on top of Kat's around the still shivering figure and whispered, "Is it safe to move her?"

"I don't see any signs of injuries. She's been drugged. We need to get her warm." Katherine saw her breath swirling in the beam of his flashlight.

Olivia was slim, and Jake lifted her easily, carrying her up the stairs to the living room. As Katherine climbed the stairs, she heard the wail of sirens in the distance. She slipped once, looked over her shoulder, and involuntarily shuddered. It was the same image she had seen in her dream. But this time, there was no pile of bodies to run away from.

32

Everyone gathered in Olivia's hospital room at Mr. Ames request. Olivia lay in bed, her face pale, with a bandage around her head. She had sustained a concussion and developed hypothermia after hours of being locked in the freezing cellar. Katherine sat on a stool at the foot of Olivia's bed. Jonathan and Robert sat side by side next to Olivia, their hostility melted by their shared love for this woman.

"A few years after my sister moved away," Jonathan started, his voice tinged with regret, "I received an invitation to Vera's wedding. But that was when Della was in the throes of kidney failure. I sent a gift, but couldn't attend."

He paused, gathering his thoughts. "After that, there was no contact with either Vera or Victor. I wasn't even aware that Vera had a daughter."

Jake, standing with Lee on the other side of the room, offered a solemn nod. "These things happen; families drift apart."

Jonathan sighed heavily, "Victor's birth ... well, it wasn't easy for my sister. She was only sixteen. Our parents wanted her to abort him, but she chose not to. I supported her and helped her get back on her feet. I don't think Victor ever knew."

He glanced out the window, lost in memories. "For Victor, it seemed like the entire 'Ames Family' resented him. He grew up without a father figure, other than me, only ten years his senior. Linda lived a wild life. I tried to be there for her, but it wasn't enough. When Ames Enterprises took off ... Apparently Victor followed my life with envy. And he turned Vera against me."

Katherine leaned closer, absorbing every word. "He manipulated Vera into hating you too?"

Jonathan nodded sadly. "Yes. He found the card I sent for Vera's wedding, with cash and a piece of family jewelry. He stole it and made her believe I wanted nothing to do with them. I was offended when Vera never acknowledged my gifts, especially the heirloom. So, I stopped trying to reach out."

As Mr. Ames grew quiet, Lee shared what he'd learned from the FBI. "Bailey Anderson has been living in Wilmington for six years. Current figures set his total take at $1.34 million from salary padding and invoice fraud. When his scheme was discov-ered last fall, he came back to Baltimore and told his sister he'd been fired. He used that and her fear of poverty to provoke her into being his accomplice in the kidnapping. Vera didn't know about the financial fraud, or Victor's plan to frame Mr. Ames."

"Vera is afraid of her brother, too. It's going to take a lot of courage for her to testify against him." Katherine shook her head. "He's been planning and scheming against you all these years. But why did he target Olivia?"

Mr. Ames sighed, "He found her on Facebook, learned about her life. Then he hired a private detective to track her movements, where she lives, who she spends time with."

"Marty," Katherine said.

Jonathan's eyes darkened. "I still don't understand why I never got the ransom note. Victor said he left it on Olivia's books on her desk. Of course, when he called me, I pretended that I got the note and was waiting for his call. Then he told me to write down a bunch of numbers and instructions. And I realized he was trying to frame me for Bailey Anderson's crimes."

Olivia's eyes fluttered open, and she took a deep breath. Everyone smiled. Jonathan kissed his daughter's hand, tears filling his eyes. Robert brushed the hair away from her face.

The detectives said their goodbyes and stepped out into the hallway. "So, Jonathan was right all along," Jake said. "Olivia did fall victim to a con artist."

Katherine smirked. "I'm afraid so. He just didn't realize it was a member of his own family."

"When did you put the pieces together, Kat?" Lee asked.

She smirked. "There were lots of clues, but the final piece clicked when I realized that Marty didn't follow Olivia on New Year's Eve."

Jake looked at her quizzically.

She chuckled as they continued down the hallway. "Robert chased him off, so Marty never went to Bailey's Bar. But you said Victor recognized Marty's picture and even said he was there asking questions that night."

Jake broke into a huge grin. "Well, Victor is still blaming Vera, but he would have no way of knowing that Marty was following Olivia unless he is the one who hired him."

Katherine began to chew her lower lip as she followed Lee and Jake into the cold night air. Something Jake said was nagging at her. There were still too many loose ends left hanging. What had happened to the ransom note? How did Olivia's books end up at the library? And what happened to the spare key to Olivia's apartment door?

"Between Olivia's testimony and the evidence we've turned up, the district attorney will have a solid case." Lee waved as he hopped on the bus that would take him home.

Jake and Katherine continued to his Jeep. Staring out the window, Katherine's mind raced. Suddenly, the final puzzle piece clicked into place. Someone else had known something they shouldn't have known. Someone else had been in Olivia's room the day she was abducted, and Katherine thought she knew who and why.

33

Katherine and Jake stood outside an apartment in one of
JHU's student housing buildings. Jake knocked again, louder.

Finally, the door opened, and a fair-skinned man with
shaggy red hair looked out at them. His usual cocky stance
slumped slightly when he saw the detectives. His eyes
narrowed.

Katherine spoke firmly. "We need to speak to you, Mr. Jones.
I think there's something you need to tell us about Olivia Ames'
kidnapping."

The previously haughty grad student slumped further and
hung his head. He opened the door to let them in, then slammed
the door loudly behind them. He crossed him arms and
dropped into a nearby bean bag chair, reminding Katherine of
an impu-dent teenager.

"I've been in the program for four years. Four years!"
Gordon leaned toward Katherine, his eyes wide. "In less than
two years, Olivia has made more progress than I ever could."

"You wanted to know what was giving her the edge?"
Katherine asked when he slipped into sullen silence.

"Yeah. I think, if I can just get a glimpse of her notes, I'll be able to get ahead of her in the project and present the new idea like it's my own. I knew she always goes home to visit her father over the weekend. I planned to go to her apartment, borrow her notes and books, and return them before she comes home.

"So, I went to the apartment Friday night, expecting Olivia to already be gone, but she's still there. I wait in the car until I see her light go out. Then she comes out with some guy following her, carrying her suitcase. They get in a car and drive off. Then I go into the building, find the spare key, and slip into her room. There's a mess of books and notes all over her desk, so I scooped them all up into the bag I brought with me."

"You didn't notice anything strange about any of the notes?" Jake asked. "Different paper, different handwriting?"

"No, man. I was trying to get in and out fast. I didn't want anyone to know I was there, so I didn't turn on the lights. I just brought a flashlight with me."

"Okay. What next?" Katherine prodded.

"I got out of there. Back in my apartment, I started flipping through her notebook and the books. Her notes were all over the place. I stayed up all night trying to make sense of them. I made notes of my own, but I couldn't figure out how she came to her conclusions. Saturday, I went through the books, but half of them didn't seem to relate to our project and they were filled with so many random notes...I started to realize what a terrible idea it all was. I could never pass off one of Olivia's discoveries as my own. My mind just isn't wired like hers."

"A little late to be realizing that." Jake's voice was sharp.

"Yeah. Well, I decided I was going to take everything back, and hope she didn't notice anything. I didn't get any sleep that night worrying about it. I went back to her apartment Sunday, thinking I could return everything. But the police were there searching the apartment. I freaked out and ran away. I wiped my fingerprints off the books, just in case, and put them in the return slot at the library."

"What did you do with the notebook?"

Gordon sighed. "I thought about throwing it away, but…" He bent over and pulled a lock box out from under his bed. He removed a red composition notebook. He held it in his hands for a moment before handing it over to Katherine.

"I couldn't do it. I hate Olivia. But her theories…" He sighed. "They will revolutionize the industry. I was surprised when I didn't hear anything about the theft, but when you showed up asking about Olivia's whereabouts, I couldn't believe my luck. She must have run away with her boyfriend, which means her research is fair game."

"Why didn't you tell us about seeing her leaving with a man that night?" Jake snapped.

"Chill out, man. I thought she was running away with her boyfriend. Why would I tell you that?"

"Because you found the ransom note."

Both men stared at Katherine after she made her pronounce-ment. Gordon 's face flushed.

"The kidnapper said he left a ransom note on top of Olivia's notebook." Katherine fanned the pages of the book in her hands and shook her head. "Where is it?"

Gordon pointed to his desk. "The drawer."

Jake pulled open the desk drawer. Aside from a few scattered office supplies, there was a large folded white sheet of paper. As he picked it up, a key fell to the ground. He handed the paper to Katherine and picked up the key.

The note was made up of words cut out of the newspaper and glued to a sheet of plain white copy paper. "We have your daughter. No police. Call me."

"There's a phone number here," Katherine said. "I bet it belongs to Victor."

Jake held up the key. "Olivia's spare key?"

Gordon looked at his hands. "From above her door. I put it in my pocket without thinking."

"Why didn't you tell anyone about finding a ransom note?" Katherine pressed.

"I didn't want to admit I'd been there!"

"Then why not take the books and leave the note on the desk?" Jake asked.

Gordon put his head in his hands. "Fine. Okay…I saw Olivia and a guy leaving the apartment with a suitcase. Then I get in there and see this crazy note. Look at it! Like something out of a movie! I'm thinking, no way that's real. I figure O and boy toy are trying to squeeze money out of daddy so they can live the good life together without his approval. Happens all the time."

"In movies." Katherine and Jake spoke at the same time.

"Maybe. But I did think that. I took the note, thinking one, it would screw Olivia over not to get the money from her dad. And two…I kept it in case she came back and accused me of stealing her research, I could hold that note over her and keep her quiet."

Katherine pocketed the note and key and frowned. "Mr. Jones, I don't even know what to say to you. I'm not sure how many crimes you've committed, but I know that you are going to be held responsible for them."

"You can't turn me in! It will ruin me." A spark of fear entered Gordon 's eyes.

Katherine waved her hand. "You should have thought of that before you made these choices. I'm going to give you the chance to turn yourself in..." Jake stiffened, but Katherine held up a calming hand.

"One chance, Mr. Jones. Turn yourself in tonight, or I will turn you in tomorrow. And Jake here is going to be parked outside this building watching you."

Jake relaxed with a nod. "Right. And if you try to go anywhere other than police headquarters, I will bring you in myself."

Gordon's face drained of all color as the detectives got up and left the room.

The detectives walked out of Gordon's apartment, the chilly air a welcome relief after the tense encounter. The streets were quiet and the city lights glistened on the wet pavement. They walked side by side to Jake's Jeep, the weight of the case finally lifting from their shoulders.

"Well, that's one more off the streets," Jake said, breaking the silence.

Katherine nodded, her thoughts still tangled in the events of the week. "Yeah, it feels good to close this one out. Olivia's safe, Victor's behind bars, and Vera is talking."

Jake glanced at her. "Don't forget that Jonathan has been cleared. The Ames Enterprises fraud case has been solved. And a bio-terrorism ring has been busted wide open." They stopped and he put his hands on her shoulders, gently turning her to face him. "You did great, Katherine. You really did."

She smiled faintly. "Thanks, Jake. I couldn't have done it without you."

"You know, Katie, I was really proud of the way you handled our interactions with Robert. I know that was hard."

Katherine sighed, feeling a heavy weight in her heart despite the relief from closing another case. "The panic attacks, the memories. It's all coming back."

Jake's expression was serious, but compassionate. "That's why I think you should talk to someone. Here." He reached into his pocket and pulled out a business card, handing it to her.

Katherine took the card, reading the name: Dr. Emily Reed, Psychologist. She shook her head.

"She's the best in the business," Jake said. "She's fully vetted and cleared. She's helped a lot of operatives work through their trauma. And she can help you too."

Katherine stared at the card, the thought of opening up to another therapist both daunting and appealing. She'd spent two years in grief counseling after Daniel's death. But her experiences this week proved she still had work to do.

Jake beamed as he walked to the driver's side. "You're strong, Katherine. You've faced a lot and come out the other side. But there's no shame in getting help to deal with the scars."

Katherine looked at him, grateful for his support. "Thanks, Jake. I'll think about it."

As Katherine hopped a bus back to her car, she slipped the business card into her pocket. She felt a small spark of hope mingled with excitement. She loved being a private detective. But she couldn't deny the extra taste of adventure that came from working with the intelligence community. With her friends' support and professional help, maybe she would follow Jake's example and consider consulting. *I wonder what kind of assignment the agency would give me?*

Later that Day...

Beth walked out of the Cut Right Salon with a spring in her step. Her usual stylist, Susan, was on vacation. But the owner, Leslie, had given her personal attention. And Beth felt great.

She looked at herself in her car's vanity mirror. Placing her hand on her stomach, she smiled smugly. *Good news from the doctor too.*

Beth pulled away from the strip mall and headed east on Fredrick Avenue. The street lamps had begun to glow and traffic thinned as people found their way home. But not Beth. She had more business to attend to tonight.

The Walters Art Museum was dark when she arrived. Beth was surprised to see Misty Vanderlin's car in the lot. A flash of envy threatened to ruin Beth's good mood. Misty had it all. Her own parking space. Curator at the Walters. Respect in the community. A wealthy husband.

A loud beeping drew Beth's attention. Misty was running across the parking lot toward her car. She jumped in and pulled away immediately. Beth smiled. She enjoyed seeing her boss upset. She placed both hands on her stomach and took a deep breath. She was going to give James the one thing his wife couldn't.

Primping her hair one last time, Beth stepped into the cold evening air and rounded the corner to the museum's employee entrance. Dim security lights guided her through the breakroom and the main exhibit halls. She finally arrived at a heavy wooden door at the back of the museum's small Neoclassical exhibit.

The door had been closed for weeks as a new exhibit was being set up. The official unveiling for museum patrons was still a week away. Beth had hoped to be the one to show it to James, but of course, Misty had beaten her to it. Beth took a deep breath as she found the large key required to open the old-fashioned lock. She was surprised her lover wasn't already there waiting for her. Misty wouldn't be James' wife much longer, not if she had anything to say about it.

The door slid into the wall with a groan and Beth stepped into the room. A glass ceiling arched twenty feet high, letting in a gentle moonlit glow. The walls around the room were lined with Baroque portraits. Beth reached to her left to raise the lights and get a better look at the exhibit she had helped assemble.

A partial wall in the middle of the room held the centerpiece of the collection, a striking 17th-century oil on canvas, *Judith Decapitating Holofernes*. The wall had been painted a deep green to accentuate the large painting's dark shadows, flickering candlelight, and dramatic content. Under the painting, an Italian table from the Baroque Era supported a small bronze statuette depicting Prometheus chained to a rock. But Beth's attention was drawn to the item at the bottom of the display. Wedged under the table in an unnatural position, the body of James Vanderlin surrounded by a pool of his own blood.

The police have arrested
James Vanderlin's murderer.
Or have they?

Coming in 2025

**Subscribe to my Newsletter at
AmethystDrake.com**

About the Author

Amethyst Drake is a passionate storyteller. She excels at crafting delightful characters and enjoys developing com-plex relationships among them. Mystery has always been her favorite genre to read, making it a natural choice for her writing. She aims to blend her personal experience with mental health and the moral complexities of intricate interpersonal relationships into engaging novels.

Amethyst loves reading all kinds of mysteries, suspense, and thrillers and enjoys watching classic detective and espionage dramas like "Murder, She Wrote," "Perry Mason," and "Mission: Impossible."

She also loves hearing from readers! Connect by signing up for her newsletter at amethystdrake.com or email amethyst@agswordsmiths.com.